Wild Oat MILK

ELENA DAWNE

Edited by fucking legend: Sotia the Awesome.

Indie published Amazon ISBN: 9798877101425

WARNING!

If you're afraid to get wet, then this book is not for you.
The content is written to *excite* and *delight*.

This is a work of FICTION.
That means I made it all up for the sake of glorious smut
— so if you think you recognize some person or place in
this book, you either have some spicy-ass friends or an
extremely active fantasy life.
I *applaud* you!

This book is also intended for ADULTS.
If that's not you, Sweet Pea, then I love your moxie, but
close the book and come back once you've turned
eighteen. X

1

JEM

The television is on, but Dad's gaze is on the framed photo next to it, where my other father's joyful face is proof that the past was as happy as we all thought. Or maybe Gabe was fooling us even then. Faking his smiles until he grew tired of us and left.

I clear my throat again. "*Dad.*"

It takes three more times before he looks my way, and when he does, he's as absent as the man in the photo.

"I'm heading next door, to babysit," I say. Not that he particularly cares where I am or what I'm doing. All he does these days is stare at that photo. He doesn't notice much when I'm around, so it's unlikely he'll notice I'm gone.

I mean, I turned eighteen last week, and it was the second birthday I've had that's gone under the radar. No *happy birthday, Jem.* Not even a whisper. Just a too-little, too-late call from Gabe on the wrong day, which I didn't bother to answer. Call me *twice shy*, because I refuse to risk being abandoned by the man more than once.

Dad turns and nods at me, like he's heard what I said. Then his gaze drifts back to the news, as if he has the capacity to pay attention to anything happening in the world today.

I sigh at his glazed expression and lack of energy. I once loved Gabe with all my heart too, but he left, and no amount of apologizing is going to make me forgive him. I hate him for what he did to our family, and every time I look at Dad, I reaffirm that I don't ever want to fall in love or depend on anyone the way he did Gabe.

My neighbor gets it. She's single on purpose. Independent and thriving, as she creates the family and life she's always wanted. Time and again, I look at how freely she lives and think, *That's what I want.*

So many times I've needed guidance and asked myself, *What would Shelby Cooper do?*

The answer is always something empowering and inspiring. She makes me feel like I'm capable of anything — I just need to figure out what I want.

I knock on her door and call out that I've arrived, and her voice rings down the stairs. "Come on in, Jem. We'll be down in a sec."

I help myself to a grape from a fruit platter on her kitchen counter, and stand taller when she comes into view with little Jaxon on her hip. "You look amazing," I say, admiring her shimmery dress with envy. "Where are you off to?"

Shelby grins and hands Jax over, so she can finish putting on her dangling earrings without his trying to rip them from her ears. "You like?" she asks with a twirl. "I'm going to down margaritas at that new line-dancing place, and snag a good-ol' country man, who'll want to go for coffee after — and by *coffee*, I mean *sex*, because I want a warm body large enough to give me cuddles, and a grown man grabbing at my tits instead of a needy little baby." She giggles and tickles Jaxon's chubby feet until he grins and squeals and kicks.

She's always so... open and shameless.

Shelby Cooper knows what she wants, she knows how to get it, and she doesn't give a shit if anyone judges her for it. She's kind of my hero.

"Well, good luck," I say. "I wouldn't know where to start with any of that," I admit with a snort, as I jiggle her ten-month-old on my hip. "The boys at school bugged the hell out of me, and I'm just grateful I don't have to see them anymore. I still can't understand how half of them got accepted into colleges on the three brain cells they shared between them when two of those neurons were so clearly focused on getting their dicks sucked. Blows my mind." I make a silly face at Jaxon. "You're the only cutie-patootie boy I'll suffer, kid."

Shelby watches me with a smile. "He's definitely my fave. But a decent roll in the hay with a grown man gives me tingles, and tonight, I need me some tingles," she says. Her gaze lingers on my knitting bag a moment, and she draws her brows down a little. "How's your dad doing?"

I shrug, because what can I say? It's been nearly two years, so it's hard to know if things are going to improve at all. None of the antidepressants Dad tries seem to touch his melancholia, and I'm not sure he'll ever be okay again.

"Have you heard much from your friends?" Shelby

asks. "It's got to be hard, staying home to take care of David, when everyone else has left for college."

I shake my head. "Honestly, I didn't have that many friends, and the few I had were in a hurry to leave town and move on before I was free to. Technically, I skipped a grade, so a gap year isn't the end of the world, and I'm not even sure college is the right path for me, so it's more financially viable if I take the time, to be sure," I say with certainty. "And I don't mind staying home," I add. "It's not like I begrudge Dad his grief and mental fragility. He'd take care of me if things were reversed." The words leave my mouth automatically, but I only half-believe them. I used to be sure of his love, but it's hard to be certain anymore. I haven't felt it in so long. If I think about it too much, it's hard to believe anyone cares, when even my parents have literally or figuratively abandoned me.

Am I the problem?

"You should come over more often," Shelby says interrupting my thoughts. Her expression is filled with concern. "I worry about you. Maybe I could take you out sometime?"

I laugh softly. "To meet country men and have *coffee*?"

"If you want." She winks.

I laugh harder, and then moan. "I do want to try *coffee*, but I'm..." I gesture at myself and shrug. "I don't think I'm anyone's type. And knowing my luck, I'd snag some useless-in-bed guy, who'd ruin the idea of sex forever. Or I'd accidentally seduce a kidnapper or some-thing, and then who'd take care of Dad?"

Shelby chuckles too, but then she gets all serious and thoughtful. "You're definitely somebody's type, Jem, but my advice would be to find an older guy, for your first time. Someone who looks and feels good to you, who's had some practice at pleasing a woman. A sweet thing like you would have him eating out of the palm of your hand within minutes. All you'd need to do is be honest and tell him what you want — decent sex and an orgasm — and ask if he can help. You just do that as many times as it takes to get laid, but I doubt you'd get a single *no,* so be prepared to get lucky on your first try."

What she says makes way too much sense, and it sort of sounds complimentary, which puts butterflies in my stomach. "You really think so?"

She swats a hand at me. "Men can be very obliging if it suits them. I asked the cutest one I could find to put a kid in me, with the understanding that I didn't want him to stick around and cramp my style by needing to play Daddy, and the pretty, dimpled son of a bitch did it. You'd be surprised what you can get if you only ask. If you want something, you have to be brave and go get it."

I nod along, because she's obviously right, even though I feel nervous just thinking about it. "What would I wear?"

"Something from my closet." Shelby grins. "You're really considering this?"

I shrug. "Maybe. It would make me feel at least a little in charge of my life."

She studies me and gives me a tight smile. "Jem, if you want to feel in charge, then take charge. Why wait?"

She adjusts one of her breast pads, so the shape can't be seen beneath the thin fabrics of her bra and dress.

"Maybe taking a break for yourself would help your dad. It's easy for him to wallow when you're taking care of everything for him, so maybe take a step back and see if he can stand alone for a while." She frowns. "I only met your folks a few times before Gabe left, but they both clearly loved you, and I doubt either of them would have wanted you to put your life on hold the way you have. Maybe start thinking about what *you* want, Jemma Wade. You have as much right to be young and self-absorbed as anyone else your age. Put yourself first for once."

I nod and blow a raspberry on Jaxon's cute little belly when he starts to wriggle and reach for his mom. "I'll think about it, but you should get going before this guy latches back on and ruins that dress."

Shelby nods and starts gathering her phone and keys and wallet into her purse while taking out a toy car, a pair of baby socks, and a spare diaper. "I'll keep the wipes," she mumbles and puts those back in. "Condoms..." She rummages through the kitchen drawer and points to the boxes in there. "Help yourself if you ever do go hunting for dick. Men are not to be fully trusted until they prove themselves clean."

I snort softly, and she shakes her head. "I'm one-hundred-percent serious, Jem," she says. "Don't accept candies from strangers unless, they're securely wrapped."

I'm about to laugh again, but she's giving me a hard look, so I nod and swallow my amusement. "Okay."

"Good girl. Now... I have my phone, and I expressed

some extra milk, in case I don't make it back until after lunchtime, but I'll be in touch, to let you know when I'll be home. Thanks for looking after my boy." She gives him a big smooch, and then rubs her lipstick off his cheek.

"Have a good time, and don't worry about us," I say.

"We're going to have a great time. Aren't we Jaxon?" He blows a spit bubble at me and vocalizes something that sounds like an elderly goat.

I give him a nod. "Exactly."

Shelby grins, opens her front door, and pauses on the step long enough to wave at us. "You two have fun."

ONCE JAXON's fed and asleep in his crib, I look through Shelby's closet. What would I wear on a night out, to attract a man's attention?

No guy has ever looked my way with interest, so the concept is a bit foreign for me. I have to put on my *What would Shelby Cooper do?* thinking hat, and look with fresh eyes.

What do straight men like?

Tits. Pussy. Ass. The curved and hole-y trinity of alluring femininity, as Shelby would say.

I look down at my oversized grandpa-cardigan, band T-shirt, and jeans, and feel so completely shapeless it hurts — even though I was totally happy with what I was wearing only minutes ago.

I trail my fingers over one of Shelby's fitted dresses. She has so many colors, but a classic little black number keeps drawing my eye. Whenever I've seen her in it, she's looked like a million bucks, and even I wouldn't turn her down if she invited me into her bed.

Oddly nervous, I wipe my clammy hands on my jeans, and then strip out of them. I won't look anywhere near as good as Shelby, but we do kind of look similar enough that I could be her chubbier sister, so I'm hoping the dress will look okay.

I try it on and stare at myself in the full-length mirror, sort of shocked by how pretty and feminine I look. The clingy black fabric makes my curves super-obvious, and the plunging neckline reveals that I actually have too much bosom to hide. It seems a little naughty, to have so much flesh on display, but there's something hot and needy about it that has me wondering what a man would think. An older man.

A thrill runs through me, and if I think too hard about enticing a mature guy, my nerves twitter even more with an alluring kind excitement. I've always been drawn to men much older than me, and Shelby's suggestion that I snag one who'll know how to please me makes me want it so badly. I'm so used to the men in my life letting me down that I'd love to encounter someone different.

I stare at myself in the mirror, trying to absorb some of Shelby's awesomeness from her dress, to combat my insecurities.

If I want something, I shouldn't wait for it.

The dress is stunning. I feel naked and covered at the same time, and as I roll my hips to swish the skirt back and forth, I look far more sensual than I ever imagined I could. I basically see myself as a dorky, wool-obsessed grandma trapped in a teen's body, and I get on with little kids, older folks, and animals far more easily than people my own age.

But in the mirror, I'm *sexy*. It's almost impossible to believe when I'm used to seeing something more frumpy and dismissible. It's like looking at a lie, and I seriously start to loathe how virginal I am, because the Jemma in the mirror can flutter her dark lashes, flash her blue eyes, and toss her boring brown hair just as flirtatiously as Shelby can, and I want to be *that* version of myself.

I meet my gaze in the reflection.

Maybe I can be. Even if only for one night? Tomorrow, perhaps.

All I need is the dress, some makeup, and a photo ID that says I'm old enough to enter a bar and order a margarita. Then I can sit back, sip my drink, and watch the crowd until I figure out who could take my virginity with a suitable level of skill.

Hopefully, he won't run away screaming when I ask.

Another thought fills my stomach with an uneasy sensation. What if I fall in love? It can happen at first sight. Right? What if some guy steals my heart, and I wake up alone the next morning to find it shattered on the floor?

I stare at the scared girl in the mirror, look deep into her eyes, and urge her to stand taller. "Nobody can break your heart if you keep it away from them. This isn't love. It's sex. You're a strong, independent woman, and *you* get to decide how you want to do it."

I nod at my reflection. "I get everything I want, and then *I* walk away. No strings attached."

2

GUNNAR

There are times when going straight home from the grocery store isn't the best course of action, even if melting ice cream is involved. Such circumstances may include something unexpected and terrible, waiting for you in your house. A serial killer. Bad news. Radiation. A bear.

There is nothing waiting for me at my place.

Nothing.

Which is literally the most terrible thing I can think of, after seeing Kirsty strolling down the supermarket aisles, hand in hand with some other guy, and a whopping, great baby belly filling out her sundress.

Before she floated through the frozen foods section, all fruitful and glowing, I would have said I'd moved on long ago. My hounding of the checkout staff to hurry up while I did my best to hide, so I wouldn't have to face her, proves I may have some fucking feelings about the opportunities I've missed, though.

Her round belly and pregnancy curves were sexy as

fuck, and the sight of her made me wish that baby was mine, which was even more of a shock to my system.

We never had a strong enough connection to warrant this kind of yearning when we were together, but if I knew I'd feel this way about seeing her knocked up, I might not have run screaming when she mentioned settling down and having a family together.

Is seeing actually believing?

When I imagine myself holding a baby…?

My guts twist with an ache I've been ignoring since I was left to be the man of the house at the ripe old age of eight. I rose to the challenge and provided for my mom and little sister as best I could, and while it gave me bucket-loads of satisfaction to see them thrive under my care, they didn't need me so much after a while, and I reveled in the freedom I gained.

A little too much, perhaps.

I was in no rush to have that kind of responsibility again.

I definitely didn't want to make babies with Kirsty when we were together, and I don't regret breaking up — I don't even miss her company. That's not what's affecting me right now. It's more that her starting a family is making me wish *I* had something to care about. Someone to depend on me and make me feel needed and essential, instead of… pointless.

Oh God. I can feel an existential crisis coming on. I thought I had nothing waiting for me at home, but it's me. *I'm* nothing.

I groan internally, as the consequences of decades of casual flings and shallow relationships catch up with me.

The bartender asks me what I need, and I can't find my voice. I point at the beer tap in front of me, let my hands show him the approximate size of the glass I want him to fill, and then slap cash on the bar, before I stagger to the darkest corner table like I'm already drunk. Off balance from the blindsiding realization that I've been actively avoiding the life I actually want.

Have I been kidding myself all these years? Fooling myself into believing I was happy, because it felt good to get my dick wet while I remained emotionally unattached, when really I'm an asshole with one foot out the door before I even enter a relationship?

Oh *God*. I'm my father.

I'm going to die alone, and I'll deserve it.

At forty-two, I'm about halfway to dead, and with each passing moment, every wasted year of my life becomes a crushing weight.

My beer is delivered, and I nod a *thank you* and sip, as I stare at the floor on the far side of the room. I need a drink, but I don't want to get drunk. I have to drive home later.

Soon. I'll head home soon. I promised my sister I'd help get her kids to sport and dance in the morning, so I can't drown my troubles in alcohol.

But *oh my fucking stars,* do I want to lose myself in something right now.

Movement catches my attention, and I bring the swinging set of Chuck Taylor sneakers into focus. Red-and-black checker-patterned, they're hi-tops, but the laces carry a lot of slack, they aren't threaded all the way to the upper eyelets, and they're double-knotted in the loose position, like whoever's wearing them appreciates shoes with an easy-on-easy-off action, without the need to waste time on untying and retying. Smart kid.

I frown. In a bar?

I lift my gaze to the owner of the small, swinging feet and find something quite unexpected.

The pretty brunette is young but definitely not a kid, if the sizable breasts bursting out of her very low-cut dress are anything to go by.

Is she wearing a pushup bra, or are they naturally this perky and magnetic? I can't keep myself from staring, and when she dips her head to sip her margarita, her bright-blue gaze meets mine, and her cheeks flush a pretty pink.

I quickly look away, my own face heating. She may be old enough to drink a margarita, but probably only barely, and that makes her way too young for me to be ogling. I make a concerted effort to keep my gaze low. Ultra-low. Back on the floor.

She starts swinging her shoes again, which means she must have stopped at some point. Why did that happen? Her feet seem so happy when they swing. Is that why I'm getting an urge to smile? Or is it that her casual, fun-looking shoes don't make sense with her seriously hot little dress?

Her sneakers stop swinging again, and I automatically look up to see why.

It's a mistake. She's staring at me.

I take my beer and swallow half of it in a nervous gulp. Why am I nervous?

Still looking right at me, she stands and takes a step toward me.

My heart thumps even faster, and the way she walks shifts her hips from side to side almost hypnotically, exaggerating her curves with each step. The seductive movement gets my cock waking up in a hurry. I should definitely be nervous.

She rests her hand on the back of the chair opposite mine and smiles. "May I sit?"

That soft voice? These manners? Her pretty eyes and lips? The way that dress highlights her tits and hips in a way that makes me want to grip them hard and hear her gasp? The fabric clings to all the right places before falling more loosely into a short but flowing skirt that swishes above her knees. It's as playful as the fucking shoes I want to see kicked off, before she crawls into my bed and spreads herself wide for me to fuck her cute little brains out.

My dick is ready to throw himself at her feet, and my chest is forced to contain with a whole new type of panic.

My body demands I say: *Sit? Yes, please do*, but my head is screaming that I'm an idiot, who's perpetuating casual non-attachments by consorting with inappropriate-for-me women. A racing heart and a hard cock are warning signs that I'm on the verge of doing it again. With a very innocent-looking young woman, who deserves better than an aging fuckboy like me.

I beg my next breath to calm me. Maybe she's mistaken me for someone else. Maybe she's killing time while she waits for friends, or she's lost or something. She may not want anything from me. I'm pretty sure she's too young to know what she wants, *period*.

She sure as hell doesn't need me hate-fucking her

cute ass because my ex's belly is full while my heart is empty. This girl makes my dick hungry, but I ain't fucking using her as therapy for my wounded ego.

"I..." I shake my head. "No. You seem very nice, and I can give you directions if you're lost, but if you need anything else, you should sit back where you were, until someone closer to your own age catches your eye."

She pouts, and I want to tug at her bottom lip with my teeth until she hisses.

"It was me who caught *your* eye," she says, settling into an I'm-staying stance and crossing her arms in a way that thrusts her tits into an even higher and prouder position.

They're going to fall out of her dress if she doesn't watch it.

"And apparently, you're still hooked." She jostles her tits, and then dips her head so low I'm forced to shift my attention from her cleavage to her amused expression. "I don't want someone my own age," she says. "I want a man with experience, who knows what he's doing. Is that you?"

I frown and lean back, doing my best not to check her out. It's hard, because she has me curious as fuck with her unexpected streak of confidence. Young people today are different to how I remember being. "Experience doing what, exactly?" I ask, wary.

"Making a woman come, mostly." She shrugs. "No guy's ever done that for me, and I want it, so I thought I'd ask."

"I..." Rendered speechless by her frank response, I watch her closely while I finish my beer.

She sips her margarita, and I narrow my gaze at her cocktail. "How many of those have you had?"

"This is my first." She wrinkles her nose a little. "And probably my last. I got it on a whim, but I prefer beer," she adds, glancing at my empty glass. "You want another?" she offers, raising her hand, ready to summon the guy who's already wiping her old table like she abandoned it for good.

"Do I...?" I pause again, looking over the most surprising young woman I may have ever met.

She's not lost.

She knows exactly what she wants, and she's asking for it.

How can she know herself so well at such a young age, when I'm only coming to understand myself after years of experience? It's the most forward a woman has ever been with me, and I'm not used to it.

I'm a big guy, and I haven't exactly been throwing out *come hither* vibes since I arrived. With all my brooding, company-repellent thoughts, I should be intimidating as fuck.

I frown again and use my foot to push out the chair she asked to occupy. "Sit."

"Am I a fucking dog?" she asks, unimpressed.

"No. And I didn't mean to imply that. I'm just... I don't know what's happening here, and yes, I do want another beer." I wave the guy down and signal for him to bring two more, but then wince. I glance at the girl who knows what she wants. "You in the mood for anything in particular, or is the same as me okay?"

She eyes my glass, and then sits and gives the guy a

thumbs up. "I'm open to learning your preferences. I feel like we might enjoy the same things."

My eyebrows shoot up my forehead so fast, I don't even try to act cool or remember my manners. "Why in the world would you think that?"

She sucks at her teeth a moment, and then nods at my Nirvana T-shirt. "I'm a fan. Of the band. And grunge. And the whole nineties' scene, in general. Kind of wish I'd been there."

I lean in, almost certain she's serious. "Why would you want that?"

She looks at me as if it's a stupid question. "So many reasons," she says, counting them off on her fingers as she continues. "Simpler times. Deep thought, without the next-level anxiety. All those decades of post-war repressed emotions, finally being unleashed through gritty music that transcended societal pressure. Artists who rebelled against the perpetual masquerade of fake happiness by refusing to hide their messages of pain in upbeat ditties. They reached out with the truth and made every struggling human feel seen and heard and valid..."

I lean closer, eager for more, but her voice fades. She blushes, as if her passionate opinion was voiced on accident.

My dick is unreasonably hard, and I need to talk myself back from the edge, before I fall off a cliff for this girl's alluring style of honest delight.

"Were you even born in the nineties?" I mumble, trying not to stare or get trapped and crushed under the pressure of her pretty blue eyes.

"If I said *no*, would it stop you from wanting to fuck

me?" she counters without pause. She twitches one dark eyebrow, threatening to arch it at me.

Her youthful confidence pokes at the belligerent ass in me. "Who said I wanted to fuck you?"

"Your fucking eyes," she says, rolling hers. "Look — are you into having a non-judgmental conversation, where the end result is likely to be me, sitting on your cock, or not? Is the obvious age difference an issue for you? Because I already said I'm looking for an older guy, and I'm definitely old enough to take a dick if you want it to be yours." She flashes her ID at the guy delivering our drinks, before he's quite formed the mouth-shape to ask her for it. He seals his lips, sets down the beer, and backs away slowly.

"Who *are* you?" I ask, as impressed as I am confused by everything about her.

She glances at the waiter, as if she wants to kick him, then returns her attention to me.

"Call me *Shelby*," she says, thrusting her hand at me in some straight-armed, militant demand for me to shake it.

I let it linger between us a moment, before I wrap my much larger hand over hers and yank her closer so fast, she almost slips off her chair. "I'm Gunnar Scott, Shelby," I rumble in her ear. "And if you keep making me want to fuck you, I may actually do it."

She gasps softly, and my dick strains in my jeans. "Little miss, I'm not sure you understand what you'd be getting into, so I'm going to lay it out, nice and clear. I've had a bad day. I didn't realize it until tonight, but I'm on the rebound. I need to feel in control, I'm not small, and I *won't* be gentle. You'll fucking feel where I've been, for days."

Her breath stutters out of her, but instead of pulling back as I'd expect, she leans in. "Will it only be about your self-gratification, or will you make it good for me, too? If you're all talk and no pleasure, I'd rather invest my time and energy elsewhere. I want attention. And lots of it. But I'll only spread my legs for someone willing to put in some fucking effort for me."

I let go of her hand and stroke the underside of her chin with my finger, as I search her face. "Where the hell did you come from, Miss Shelby No-last-name?"

She flutters her eyelashes, and a little pinkness blooms in her cheeks. "The other side of town. And you won't be getting another name. I'm not looking to make a permanent connection, and with your being on the rebound, a one-night, no-strings-attached hookup will suit us both."

My heart is definitely feeling tender, because her fair boundary feels weirdly like a rejection. There's a subtle sting in my chest, but I nod. She's making the right call. "No strings. Fine by me. My dick will happily rise to any challenge you want to set, darlin'."

"Mmm…" She hums softly, leans back, and takes hold of her beer. "I like the way you talk, country boy."

"*Boy?* I'm probably twice your age."

She smiles and scrunches her nose at me, all cute as fuck. "Whatever. Talk some more while I drink my beer. Tell me about your breakup."

I frown hard at her. "It happened a while ago, but I saw her at the store earlier this evening and hid, so now

I'm questioning a lot of shit about my life choices, and I don't want to talk about it."

She dips one eyebrow while keeping the other level and continues, undeterred. "Just give me the reason for it, so I know if I need to be scared. Tell me it wasn't because you fucked her too hard and nasty."

I snort and shake my head. "I did, but she enjoyed that part of our relationship."

Shelby continues watching me as she drinks, her eyebrows poised to react. Is she waiting for me to give her more information?

I sigh and take a few gulps of my beer before moving it away when it tastes too good. "One of us wanted to settle down and raise a bunch of kids, and the other one didn't," I explain with a shrug.

"Which one were you?" she asks.

She's too fucking clever, this one. Could have me wrapped around her little black-nail-varnished finger in no time.

"Does it matter?" I ask back.

Why the fuck does the color of her nails excite me? Or is it the tiny silver hoop pierced through one of them that's piquing my interest? The little heart dangling from it looks like it should jingle when it swings back and forth with every movement of her hand.

"It's over," I say flatly. "It's been over for a long time. It doesn't matter who wanted to sow their wild oats."

"Women can't sow wild oats — only grow them — so I'm assuming it was you who wasn't ready to make babies." She's, still watching me, as she takes another sip of beer. "I'm not judging, but we're using condoms, so there'll be no oat-sowing here." She gestures between us.

I give her a stern look. "That's a given. We already said *no strings*. Oats are stringy as fuck."

She giggles, covers her mouth until she's swallowed, and coughs slightly. "Where do you want to do this? In the alley outside?"

"Classy," I mutter with a snort.

"Maybe I like things quick and dirty." She finishes her beer and sets her glass on the table. "I didn't trade my comfy jeans to wear this easy-access dress for nothing."

I drag my hands down my face and scratch at my beard, as I look her up and down. I shake my head. "No back-alley quickies. You demanded effort, and I'm convinced you're worth it." I stand and reach out a hand for hers. "Plus, if I lick your slit until you scream in the alley, someone will think I'm attacking you. You're young enough to need ID in a bar, but my beard is getting its first silver streaks, so I'll come off looking bad if we're caught."

She stares at me a while, then rests her hand on mine. "Where would you prefer to eat my pussy?"

"My place. The neighbors aren't so close." I lead her away from the table, before I turn back to meet her wide eyes. "I don't mean that in a dangerous way," I amend quickly when I recognize the panic in her face.

"You can do that thing where you tell a friend where you'll be and all that, if it makes you feel safer. My sister used to do that. She lives on the same street, if that helps? Not because of some weird family thing — we're not in each other's pockets or anything; it was inherited land, and we each got a slice. I'm a good guy, I swear."

I look over the sweet young thing I'm about to drag home and rebound-fuck because someone else fucked a baby into a woman I don't even like that much and I'm an inappropriately jealous meathead.

I'm going to break the poor girl, and she clearly has no fucking idea it's coming.

I drop her hand. "Fuck."

She gives me a strange sideways look, and I shoo her away with my hands. "I just realized I'm *not* a good guy. I'm a filthy old fuck, who wants to forget myself for a while, by burying my cock in a pretty girl. You're definitely far too young for me."

Her eyebrows lift. "You think I'm pretty?"

I stare at her. "Is that a trick question? Those eyes? That ass and those tits? You're fucking gorgeous. And you deserve better. Go home to your mom and pray for our souls, or something."

She drops one eyebrow and hitches the other even higher. "I'm not religious, and I don't have a mom. But you appear to have a conscience, which is more than a lot of men have, and I appreciate that. Take me home with you."

I rub at my chin and study her serious face. "You don't have a mom?"

"Two dads," she says with a smirk, before the twinkle fades from her eyes. "Well, one now." Her jaw stiffens, and she runs a hand over her stomach and fists it in the fabric of her dress. "Can we not talk about this? The loss has become a tedious daily ritual, and I'm trying really hard to feel young and carefree for the night. I want to feel alive for *one* fucking night, Gunnar."

We're both looking to forget ourselves?

I bow my head a little. "I'm sorry for your loss."

Shelby nods. She smooths out her dress and taps her fingers against her thighs, as she looks around. "Are you sorry enough to help me feel better or not?"

3

JEM

G *unnar Scott: Stonemason.*

It's written on the side of his vintage black truck, so his name checks out, at least.

This is a hot fucking ride. Chevy. From the fifties, I'd say. Not lowered and pimped-out all douche-y, either. Just all-original flair, as it's meant to be. Sleek and well-kept.

Ruggedly handsome and gruff-speaking Gunnar clearly puts some time and care into maintenance, and that excites my insides in a way I wasn't expecting. Will he rub and polish me with the same attention until I shine too?

God, I hope so. Shelby's dress has done wonders to hook a man first try, and it's boosted my confidence to a potentially dangerous state. I feel wild and invincible, like I could do anything.

I should probably message someone, to tell them who I'm with, like he said. I pull out my phone and scroll down my very short list of dependable contacts, but the

only person I could tell who'd give a shit, is Shelby, and I
can't tell her, because I stole her ID when I borrowed her
dress. She'll have questions, and while she'd totally let me
use her identity to buy a drink or two, she won't approve
of me borrowing it to seduce a man.

I hesitate for the first time all night.

Gunnar takes a few more steps, but turns back when
I don't take them with him. "I had two," he says after a
while.

The wind picks up, and I tame the skirt of my dress
as it starts to rise, trying to keep my focus. "Huh?"

"Drinks," he clarifies. "Not even two. One and a bit.
I'm safe to drive; I promise."

I nod and put my phone away. "I believe you. I was
just letting my people know who I'm with." As long as he
thinks I have people in the know, the safety system works.
Right?

He smiles. "Good. So what line of work are you in,
Shelby?"

"Oh. Um... retail," I say, not wanting to admit that
I'm burning through the family savings and babysitting
for extra cash like a fourteen-year-old girl, to keep us
afloat while I figure out how to earn a decent living while
helping Dad get back on his feet.

"What kind of retail?" Gunnar asks, probing for more
information from the vague responses I've given him
about where I work. He opens the passenger side door
for me.

Guys still do that old-school shit?

I look him over. Tall and sturdy, with fair hair and a
flannel shirt over his band Tee that brings out the vibrant

blue in his eyes, he's an enticing mix of semi-cultured, outdoor type, and I feel strangely at home in his presence. His darker-blond, mature beard bears no excessive-manscaping hipster vibes. He has playful smile-lines around his eyes, and his skin looks warmly weathered by actual sunshine, instead of giving off the cool and pasty gamer-glow my classmates tended to have.

He *is* old-school. The real deal. When he looks at me, he's actually *looking*. And thinking things about what he's seeing. He hasn't looked at his phone once, since I noticed him — I don't even know if he *has* a cellphone. His attention has been solely on me, even when it's obvious he's trying not to look at me. All of these things make him wildly interesting and appealing... I think he *likes* me.

I've slicked my thighs just from looking at him, and yeah, maybe I should have worn underwear, but what would be the point in putting up barriers, when my intention is to lose my virginity?

Gunnar Scott intends to take me home and lick my slit until I scream, and then he's going to fuck me hard with his big dick.

A shiver runs through me. I fucking believe him on all counts, and I want it.

When he pulled me in close and rumbled that I'd feel him for days, I'm sure it was meant to sound like a warning to run away, but after months of unshakeable numbness, the promise of feeling anything had only sweetened the deal. I *want* to have a lasting memory of this rite of passage. Good or bad, it will be the yardstick by which all future sexual encounters are measured, and

I'd rather have strong feelings about it, than no feelings at all. I'm so fucking sick of having to feel nothing.

Can't be happy. Can't be sad. I have to live in the fucking middle and just get shit done, because nobody else is going to do it.

Shelby was right to suggest cutting my teeth on an older guy. A capable, practiced hand. I'm tired of being the strong one. I want someone to take care of me, for a change.

"Like, what store?" I climb into his truck, and decide on another vague response to adhere to the no-strings ideal. "Nothing cool," I say when he gets in the other door and takes his place on the far side of the tan leather bench seat. "One of the clothing places in a department-store downtown. It's a living. I don't love it. What about what you do?"

I cringe and shake my head. "I mean, I can read. Your truck says, *Stonemason*. That's pretty fucking cool. Do you enjoy it? It's what you love?"

He stares at me a moment. "Why do you ask?"

I squint back. "Why don't you answer?"

He snorts softly and puts the truck in gear. "You first."

I shrug and look both ways with him, as we wait to pull out of the parking lot. "My job pays the bills, but I'd rather get paid for something I'm passionate about. I guess I'm asking for research purposes? I'm curious if anyone actually enjoys their work, because I want to believe it's possible. Consider me an ignorant youth, wondering if there's something to look forward to."

Gunnar pulls on the handbrake, shifts into neutral,

and stares at me again. "I like what I do, or I wouldn't do it. Life's too short, to waste it on things you don't believe in. If I'm not working toward the dream, then what the fuck am I doing? What are any of us doing?"

I search his face. "From what I can tell, we're all doing our best to make it through each day on blind faith that tomorrow might be better."

His searing gaze makes my cheeks feel hot. He reaches over and unlatches my seatbelt, which may be the most offensive thing that's ever happened to me. "You're kicking me out?"

He frowns. "With insights like that and tits like those? *Fuck* no."

He reaches across the seat, grabs me with strong hands, and hauls me closer, until we're breathing each other's air. "You were sitting too far away to kiss," he says, pushing his fingers into the hair at the base of my skull.

My scalp prickles with sensation as his grip firms. He pulls my mouth to his in a kiss that starts with a gentle teasing taste but quickly progresses to an authoritative and capable plundering that urges me to either resist or submit. Each of his testing passes leaves me feeling more and more needy, and I choose to chase the satisfaction he seems to promise.

He moans into my mouth and works his fingers deeper into my hair, until he's tugging and angling me to take his tongue just so. He slides his other hand down the neckline of my borrowed dress, to slip beneath the fabric and palm my breast. I gasp against his lips as he captures my nipple between his thumb and finger and twists, and then I press closer.

It's exactly what I wanted, and he knew just how to give it to me. He really does know what he's doing. I want him to show me more, and his mindful touch and mature presence gives me the courage to say so.

"Take me home and lick me," I pant when he releases my breast and pulls back with a strained sigh. "Now," I say, embracing the shameless need that he evokes in me. "I want to come."

He sweeps his tongue over his bottom lip and glances around before he runs his rough fingers up my outer thigh and under my dress. "Would you still come home with me if I made you come right here?" He grips my bare, fleshy ass with an approving grunt, and then trails his hand over to my inner thigh and thrusts my legs apart.

"Short dress and no panties. With a stiff breeze outside. Bold choice."

His gaze doesn't leave mine, and he strokes his thick fingers through my slick folds. His eyelids flicker with almost the same sort of fluttering I can feel in my chest as his eyes search mine, and he mutters under his breath. "You're soaking wet, little miss."

That name makes my legs slip wider in invitation, but he only keeps stroking. *Stroking.* So slowly, I want to growl in frustration. I rock into his touch, wanting him to push his fingers inside, the way I would have by now if they were mine.

"Why isn't your face between my legs yet?" I ask when he purposely eases back. I chase his hand, too incensed with need to mind my tongue or my actions.

His smiling lips press together, and he hums with what I'm certain is approval.

He likes me — likes the way my body responds to him and how my hungry thoughts blurt out uncensored. *Good*. Because I'm going to say and do some outlandish shit by the time we're done with each other, I just know it. I need him touching me again.

"I'm serious," I warn him, when he continues to watch me squirm instead of bringing me relief. "Get me any wetter, and you'll need to lick my slick from your seats, too."

A soft puff of air leaves his nose, as he smirks. "I like the sound of that," he says in a husky whisper.

Everything lights up bright as day around us.

I jump when a horn blasts at us from behind, but Gunnar isn't fazed.

He pushes two big fingers inside me and smothers my surprised cry with his hungry mouth. He gulps down my whimpers, like they're just what he wanted, and I urgently want to give him some more. When he hooks his fingers into my inner walls and pumps them in and out of me, I surrender to his touch, but he soon retreats, to leave me needy and bereft.

"Sorry, little miss. We need to move," he says, taking his fingers to his smiling mouth. He licks them once. Twice. And then sucks them both into his mouth, cleansing them of my arousal in the most unhurried fashion imaginable as he moans.

The horn sounds again, and Gunnar barely seems to notice. His entire focus is on me, and his pupils are so dilated I can hardly see the blue of his eyes, despite the brightness from the headlights behind us lighting up the side of his face.

"They can fucking wait," he rumbles when I glance backward. "I need some more."

I stare at him, transfixed. I don't think anyone has looked at me with this much intensity and interest since maybe when I learned to walk. Definitely not so recently I can remember the seductive feeling of being worthy or special enough to have earned the attention.

He's literally holding up traffic. For me. I'm going to give him anything he wants, I just know it. What if he wants to stick it in my ass?

"Shelby, fuck that sweet little cunt with your fingers and give me some more," he commands in a deep, gravel-like tone that makes him sound desperate for another taste. How rough would those husky whispers feel against my skin?

The only thing wrong about it is that he called me *Shelby*. Would he forgive me for the lie if I confessed right now? Or would he kick me out of his car and leave me pining for his intensely masculine energy and the flattering way he seems enthralled every time I check to see if he's looking at me.

When I don't move, Gunnar frowns. It highlights the fine lines in his forehead and reminds me of our age difference. It's somehow reassuring and intimidating all at once. He's a big, strong-looking man with years of experience, who lugs around stones, and promises to fuck me so I'll feel it for days. He's like a moderately refined caveman, only he's wearing a flannel shirt over a band T-shirt that looks like he bought it at an actual Nirvana concert. A mountain man with the heart of a musician, maybe? *Fuck*, that's a hot combo.

"Little miss?"

God, that fucking name. My heart is racing, and my breath is hard to catch. I'll be his *little miss* any day of the week, if he keeps looking at me like I'm where his next breath is coming from. I'm so going to give him whatever he wants.

He lowers his voice. "Baby girl, I asked you to do something, but maybe it was wrong of me. Am I being too pushy? Do you not want to do it?" He asks so gently, I could definitely tell him if that was the case, but it's not. I want to do what he said, and the way he's hard and forceful one minute and sweetly soft the next is weirdly hot and only makes me want it more.

I pull up the skirt of my dress and slide my hand between my legs, to fuck my juicy pussy with my fingers like he asked, while I stare at him, just as transfixed as he seems to be with me. "You didn't say *please*," I whisper.

He swallows visibly and lowers his gaze, to watch my hand's every move. "Look at my face and hear the desperation in my tone when I tell you I want more of that sweet fucking taste in my mouth. The *please* is implied, woman. *Gimme*."

The obnoxious honking comes again, long and angry this time. I collect some of my slippery mess, offer it to Gunnar, and grin when he grabs my wrist and takes my shining hand straight to his mouth.

He slides his tongue between my fingers in the most sinful fucking way.

I swear under my breath and glance out the back window, when I hear a car door slam. "Better take me home, before you get us in trouble, Gunnar Scott."

He presses his bird-flipping finger to his window and watches my face, as he suckles my fingers. He releases them slowly and deliberately, and then pushes my hand back beneath my dress. "More."

"Can I make that order to-go?" I glance at the angry face outside his window and pin my bottom lip with my teeth.

Gunnar grunts softly and pulls a different seatbelt part of the way around me, so I can push it home. "Buckle in right here, sugar-puss," he says, putting the old truck into gear again. "You're going to keep touching yourself while I drive, and I want you close, so I can feel every change in your body. If you make yourself come, I'll know, and I won't be happy about it happening without me. You went out of your way to ask me to do it for you, so your pleasure is mine tonight. Understood?"

I give an almost-nod, and he responds with a firm one of his own before pulling out into the street.

"Tell me what you're doing," he says when I shuffle around in the seat beside him.

"I'm getting comfortable." I spread my legs and tug the skirt of my dress so high, I can see my pussy reflected in the highly polished wood of the dash each time we pass under a streetlight. "You're pumping out heat like a furnace," I mutter, pressing the back of my spare hand to my cheek. I wriggle out of my denim jacket and fan myself a little.

"I run hot," he says, cracking his window.

He meets my gaze and smolders at me like a moth-erfucker.

"I believe it," I mumble when he returns his attention

to the road. Curious, I rest my hand on his thigh, and then slide it up and down, to feel the powerful muscle beneath my palm before inching my exploration higher.

"Don't touch my dick when I'm driving," he warns. "If you have to touch something, touch yourself. The wetter you are, the better you'll take my fat cock in that tight, young cunt of yours. I'm getting bigger and harder just thinking about it"

I shiver and take my hand back, so I can snuggle closer to him while I rub my clit. "I like your filthy words."

"That's why I use them," he says casually. "Scares away the prudes, and leaves me with the kind of women I enjoy. I like the way you respond to me, and you're not shy about showing me what you want. Not everyone is that beautifully honest and open. You had much dick, miss?"

I avoid his eyes and shrug. "Not a lot." That implies my pussy has had some action, but I know he doesn't mean the dick-shaped glass dildo Shelby got me for a Graduation gift. I don't think he'd take it well if I told him I was a virgin when it came to real-life cock. I doubt he'd make me feel anything for days then— probably drop me off at a church instead, given that he told me to pray earlier. I won't be admitting actual experience levels to him any time soon.

"What does *not a lot* mean to you?" he probes further.

"It means I have standards to keep, and there are a lot of creeps out there, for a young woman to sift through, so I choose to pace myself. Early days, and all that."

"Fair enough." He chuckles softly. "Tell me about what you like while you're fucking those fingers, baby girl."

I love how openly we've been talking about stuff that might make some people clutch their pearls, and I pump my fingers in and out of my pussy a little faster, loving how wet I sound. "I don't know. I like music. Knitting and crochet and stuff."

Gunnar laughs out loud. "I meant what you like in bed, Shelby. But your answer was cute as hell, and I enjoyed it as much as I'm enjoying the sound of you juicing up your fucking hand to perfection. Let me lick those pretty fingers while you tell me the kinds of things you like to knit."

I move my fingers toward his mouth, and watch him strain to reach them when I hold them just a little too far away. He grunts and grips my wrist like a lollipop stem again, which leaves him to steer with one hand, while he sucks at my fingertips. The more into me he is, the more excited I get, and the way he's savoring every lick of my arousal is making me want his tongue between my legs so badly.

I shift restlessly on his leather seat, my breath coming even faster, as I try to focus on what he asked about. "I... um... I like making little animals. Barnyard and forest creatures mostly. The cute ones. Ocean critters and predators don't excite me much."

He sucks at me harder, and then flicks his tongue over my palm and down to where his fingers are wrapped around my wrist.

Did I cover my whole hand in my arousal? Because

he's acting like I did. His lips are soft, but his beard is the slightest bit scratchy, and the sensations are all so new and foreign and utterly intoxicating.

There's a level of anticipation inside me that I don't know what to do with. I'm not sure what to expect, and the tittering excitement in my stomach is making my heart rate hustle, like it's late for something. There can't be much of my flavor left, for him to lick, but I can't tell if he'll stop, when it feels like he may keep going until he devours me. His tongue tickles, and he's making me feel so fucking edible, I want to offer myself on a platter.

"What do you do with the little creatures you make?" He brings my knuckles to his nose and inhales deeply before pressing a kiss to them.

"I... knit them little clothes, and sometimes I make them do skits for the neighbor's kid. Other times, I just strip them naked and make them fuck each other like the animals they are. Depends on my mood."

Gunnar slows to a full stop at an intersection he only needs to yield at, but there are no other cars around. Or houses. In fact, the solo streetlight illuminating us is the only one I can see.

We're on the outskirts of town?

Somehow, that makes a lot of sense when I look him over. He does seem a little bit country and a little bit rock 'n' roll.

"I think I'd like to see that," he says before taking another pull on my fingers.

"My knitting?"

His eyebrows shrug a *yes*, while his tongue is busy, flicking over my palm again.

My cheeks warm, and I try not to read too much into his response. I doubt he's serious about being interested in my hobbies. He probably thinks I'm a weirdo for playing with my creations, like everyone else who knows I do it. Well, except baby Jaxon, who laps that shit right up.

"What would you like to see, exactly, Mr. Scott?" I ask. "The sweeter of the woolen-puppet activities or the sexy ones?"

"Both," he says, his eyes sparkling. "I also want to see these." He traces the plunging V neck of my dress with his fingertips, and with two expertly timed flicks of his wrist, he coaxes each breast from the flimsy fabric, exposing my firm and needy nipples to the open air.

"I like these." He leans in and elicits a gasp from me, as he suckles gently at my breast. It feels amazing, and when he moves to take my other nipple into his mouth, I practically thrust it at him. He smiles into my flesh, and then tugs hard enough with his mouth to force a needy moan from my lips, before he pulls away. My nipple throbs at his departure, and his fingertips play a subtle caress over my sensitive skin, where his beard has left it tingling. "Tell me some things you like, darlin'," he says in a husky whisper.

"I like your beard," I say without thinking too hard. "I want to feel it brushing at me while you suck my tits some more, and I want you to scrape it along the insides of my thighs. And down my stomach. Along my back. All over, really. It's softer than I thought, but still rough, and my skin's still trying to make sense of the juxtaposition."

"That's a big word, for a little thing." His smile teases

me, as he gently tugs one of my nipples between his fingers in a way that makes my pussy want more attention.

"Well, I may be younger and smaller than you, but I'm also a big fucking dork, and big words come with the territory. It means—"

"I know what it fucking means," he growls, giving my other nipple a sharp tug. I expected it to hurt, like a punishment, but it's the opposite. It's like my nipples are a dial that turns up the volume of my need, and Gunnar's intentionally driving me toward more pleasure. He twists and squeezes until my nipple is hot and pulsating and making my thighs twist together, while my surprised breaths become pantings of desire.

"Just because I work with rocks, doesn't mean my head's full of them," he says, his voice low and gritty by my ear. "Maybe I'm a dork too. Maybe I like to fuck sexy little nerds and trade magniloquent words under the covers, after we've said all the simple, filthy things that needed to be said first."

"*Magniloquent?*" I ask breathily, thrusting my chest at him in a demand for more of his expert touch. "And I thought you were hot before."

Gunnar drops his gaze to my hand as I rub my clit faster.

I can't believe I'm being so fucking brazen, but I like the way he looks at me when I'm touching myself, and he did ask me to do it.

Masturbation isn't something I'd usually admit to doing — let alone flaunting — but it's something sexual I'm familiar with, and when facing a man of obvious experience, I kinda want to feel like a pro at something too. Since fucking myself is basically the only thing in my life that feels good, I do it often enough that I *am* a pro, and from the absolute focus he's giving me, Gunnar admires my abilities.

I want him to take me home and pay even closer attention to me.

"How much longer to your place?" I rock on my ass and push four fingers inside, to feel the stretch, as I tug at my other nipple.

"Nearly there," he rumbles, putting his truck in gear. "Don't you fucking come, or I'll spank that gorgeous ass. I want you coming on my tongue the first time."

"*First time?*" My pussy twitches in a threatening release. "You're going to make me come more than once?"

He chuckles and shakes his head, as he follows a winding country road uphill. "Oh, baby girl, it's going to be a good and long night."

4

GUNNAR

I'm so fucking excited and hard when I pull on the handbrake, I almost wrench the thing right off.

Shelby's been fucking herself, with her tits out, all the way up my mountain, and her scent is doing my fucking head in. She's everywhere, permeating my nostrils and infiltrating my brain to the point of madness.

I've had little taste tests, but I'm dying to feast on her, and she practically yelps when I tear off her seatbelt and skin her dress from her body.

Her wide eyes gaze up at me in surprise, and I groan and try to remember myself. "Baby girl, I told you I'd be rough, but I'm not a monster, and I don't want to hurt you in a bad way. If you need me to back off, you just say the word."

She pants at me, her full, round breasts begging for attention with each rise and fall of her bare chest. "Like a *safe* word?"

I step out of the truck, grab her leg and spin her so she's laid out on my '54 Chevy's bench seat. Her breath hitches, but she props her sneakered little feet on the leather and slips her hand back between her legs, looking up at me, all adorable and sexy at the same time. She's so fucking young, and I want to shove my cock in her so bad.

What the fuck is this shit?

I've only ever dated women close to my own age, but this girl... She's about the freshest meat off the market, and I'm fucking *loving* it. My ego feels invincible that she's offering her body to me, but I'm almost positive I should feel guilty for giving in to such sweet temptation.

Am I overcorrecting for my thoughts about wanting to settle down? Running from the idea of family again? Chasing the empty detachment of a one-night stand with a stranger so far from that stage of her life I can't possibly get what I want from her?

My pretty girl tugs at one of her nipples, gazing up at me with such trust and interest, I don't fucking care to think anymore.

I only want to feel, because I know how good she's going to taste, and how fucking big and important and appreciated I'm going to feel when I push inside her and make her come the way she wants to.

She shivers, as I trail my fingers down her soft stomach.

"You don't need a special word, darlin'," I assure her. "All the words are safe with me. I like to take the lead, but I'm not into punishment or pretending. I'm a big boy, who likes to get excited, and you're allowed to demand I fuck you harder or to settle down. You tell me how it is, and I'll listen," I say, leaning in.

I extract her glistening hand from her cunt and push

it into my hair, making her fingers curl into a fist. I want to smell of her everywhere by morning. "If your thighs clamp over my ears so hard I can't hear you, and you need my attention, you pull my hair. Got it?"

Pretty blue eyes still huge, she nods.

"Good girl," I say with a grin.

She whimpers softly and rocks her hips, and I pull her ass closer. Looks like my girl enjoys some praise, and she's been behaving beautifully, so she's definitely going to get more.

This is going to be fun.

I run my hands up and down her soft thighs. My palms delight in her smoothness and the size of them look huge on her. I feel so big in comparison to this young beauty, and it makes my cock even harder when I recall how tight she was around my fingers earlier. A powerful thrill runs through me, as I think about stretching her young pussy to accommodate me. Will I even be able to get myself in? I'll get her fucking dripping, so she can take every fat fucking inch. *God*, she's going to squeeze me so beautifully.

I'm loving the feel of her in my hands. She's sturdy enough for rough fucking, and she's got a substantial rack, sexy-as-fuck breeder's hips, and a good, meaty ass on her, but she's not a tall woman, and it has me feeling a little drunk with the power difference. When I picture her on her knees for me, it gives me god-like vibes, and that's a fucking potent aphrodisiac.

My dick is leaking so much pre-cum, it's seeping through my jeans. I want to pull her into my lap and make her ride the wet spot until her juices soak through to me.

Maybe I'll do that next.

I grip her legs, lift, and spread them, until her pussy lips part and I can see her tight little holes lined up and shining in the moonlight. So fucking pretty.

With a smile, I lean in close and breathe in her scent, rumbling in approval as she trembles in my hands. Mouth open, I run my face through her slit, coating the surface of my tongue with her arousal, and I savor her taste as I would a melting candy, before swallowing down her sweetness.

A surge of craving washes over me with an intensity I didn't expect. I latch on to her clit, and she gasps, but her breathy sighs quickly turns into mewling moans when I start to suckle. I tug her little bud into my mouth and keep the suction on, while I flick at it with the tip of my tongue.

She squirms beautifully. Her entire body gets involved, and when she squeezes her thighs around my head, I thrust them back open and make her take a little more pressure.

Her hips jerk, and she tries to buck, but I pin her to the leather seat and get her whimpering and grabbing fistfuls of my hair. She doesn't use her grip to tear me away; she pulls me closer, lifting to me in slow, rolling thrusts that make me want to feel her under my hips, while I rock my thick cock into her heat.

Not yet.

We've got all night.

One night only. No strings attached. And I'm going

to make the most of every fucking second, before I slap her ass and send her on her way. The thought of not seeing her again strikes me like a loss, but I shake it off. Tonight is *not* the night to explore or resolve my sudden lonely-heart crisis and my building urge to start a family. What am I going to do? Tie her down and breed her?

I take a moment to gaze at her pretty little cunt, imagining myself filling it with cum. It's fucking tempting, but that's not what we agreed. One night of fun. That's all this is.

I nuzzle into it, and her moan is so rewarding, I have to do it again, and again, until she gushing into my beard and shifting her ass around so much, I want to push something inside it. Has she done that before? She's young, but she's bold, so maybe. Or would I be her first?

The thought makes my balls ache, and my dick is so cramped inside its denim cage, I have to tear my jeans open, to give it the space to quit throbbing. Liberation doesn't ease the lusty ache, though; it gives it room to grow.

I raise her legs higher, and plunder her juicy little cunt with my tongue, until she forgets to contain her volume and starts swearing loudly and crying out just the way I like.

"That's it, baby girl. Let me hear how good you feel," I rumble at her, as I drag some of her slick to her puckered little ass. I fuck her cunt with my tongue and rub at her tight little asshole, until her grip in my hair is driving me to push her even harder. The tension in her body is growing by the second.

I want to be inside her. Inside this perfectly delicious,

fuckable little miss. Not just my tongue, but also my cock. My *seed*. Fuck, I want to pin her down, shoot my load in her, and watch it slowly trickle back out.

The overwhelming urge to breed her slams into me so hard, it makes me growl into her pussy in frustration. It's riding my ass, pulsing in my balls, and my cock is dripping with the desire to fuck a baby into this pretty, young woman.

I swipe my thumb over my knob, collecting pre-cum, and then take it to her asshole and push it inside her, as if she's mine to fucking smear. I know it's wrong to do without asking, but I'm clean, and it's not like I'm making any babies up her cute, twitchy little ass.

Shelby bucks at my face, apparently loving the way I'm nudging my thumb up her back hole while I lick her soaking cunt. She rocks and writhes and makes the cutest fucking noises that push my patience too far. Eager to see her cresting, I spear my tongue inside her and fuck her ass with my thumb until her snug little cunt squeezes at me.

She gushes hot, salty juice into my mouth, and I gulp down her cum, moaning almost as much as she is, to express how fucking pleased I am. Pleased and tortured with the need to get her inside and push her down on my bed, to fuck that squirty little cunt.

I barely wait for her to come down from her orgasm, before I drag her out of the truck and throw her over my shoulder. I slap her ass, just to see it jiggle, and then again when she starts to squirm, all sexy and needy.

I slap her right on her pussy, and she cries out. She

grips me hard, pants the sweetest whimpers, and clenches her ass cheeks.

"Are you coming again, baby girl?" I ask.

She utters softly. "Almost."

I chuckle and take her inside. "You want me to spank you till you get off?"

"Is that a thing?" She kicks her sneakers a little, like she might be excited by the idea, and I throw her down onto my bed with a grin.

"It is if you want it to be," I say, getting shirtless. My dick is only getting harder at the thought of my hand rouging her round buttocks, and with my jeans open the way they are, she's well aware of my appreciation.

She gazes up at me, eyes flashing and cheeks rosy. She seems totally unfazed by her nudity as she takes me in, and it's intoxicating. I've never been with a woman who wasn't at least a little shy about her body to begin with, and it's refreshing as hell to have someone confident right from the start.

I seize one of her feet, tug off her shoe, and toss it behind me, as I stare at her stripy sock. I point at it. "Did you knit this?"

She gives a small nod and covers her eyes.

I pull off her sock with a smile. "Please explain to me how you can be more shy about a sock than you are about my thumb fucking your ass while I drink from your sweet little pussy."

Her cheeks grow even rosier, and she reaches around, grabs a pillow, and covers her face with it, to hide as she groans.

I reach for her other shoe and remove that, too. The

sock on this foot has a different pattern, but I think it's on purpose, because the spots are the same colors as the stripes were on the first one.

"Well, aren't you just the cutest little dork? It kind of feels like spanking that cute ass of yours too much would make glitter sparkles and unicorns fall out." I hum with approval, flip her over, and slap her ass so sharply, she yelps. The shape of my hand develops quickly on her pale ass, branding her skin pink, and when she raises her hindquarters in a quiet plea for more, I want to launch myself at her and stuff my fat cock in her young cunt.

"*Fucking hell*, little miss. You're making me want to fuck you so damn hard. I need to calm down, before I lose my shit and break your sweet little pussy. You want a drink?" I head back to the kitchen, to wash my hands and get a fucking grip on myself, because I definitely want to rough-fuck her until my dick is coated in glitter or some shit.

I want to fuck her all night, like I want to make those sparkles permanent. For some reason, the thought of having a bedazzled cock is getting my balls seriously tight, and if I don't pace myself, we'll both run out of steam before I've given her the night of her fucking life.

I pause as I'm pouring whiskey into a tumbler.

Night of her life? What the fuck am I doing?

Am I trying to make sure she comes back?

I look behind me, as she walks boldly out of my bedroom and toward me.

"What kind of drink?" she asks, leaning on tiptoes to glance over my shoulder.

"Whiskey? Water? Something else? What would you like?"

If I don't have it, I can jump back in the truck and get whatever she asks for, because — *holy fuck* — I do want her to come back. I've never met anyone like her, and I don't care if she's half my age, I —

I drag a hand down my face and moan. I'm in so much fucking trouble. I want to tie her to my bed and eat cunt-coated candy from her pussy, forever. What the fuck is wrong with me?

"Scratch that. Whiskey or water," I say in my firmest tone. "That's all you can have."

Her eyebrows dip in the center, and she looks me over. "I want both, then. And a shot of cum."

I gape at the sharp tone of her demand, but I disguise it by scratching at my beard while I shove my jaw closed. I drink in her sassy hip, moody pout, and unimpressed eyebrow, and then give her a low whistle. "I'll give you a shot of cum in your ass if you need it, little miss. Come get your whiskey and don't sass me in my own home. Tell me why you just got snippy."

Her face pulls tight. She sighs, goes back into my bedroom, and stomps out again, while pulling my *Nirvana* T-shirt on over her head. "You were being nice, offering me choices, and then you got grumpy and took them away," she says once she's glaring at me again. "How am I meant to respond?"

I look down at her feet. She's standing pigeon-toed; her toes curled into the wooden floor, huddling together like cold little critters during a snowfall. Rainbow-colored ones. Her toenails are painted every color there is. Is that a *Pride* statement for her dads? And if it is, why would she hide them in her shoes? What kind of statement is that? One for herself? Or am I overthinking it, and it's not any kind of statement at all? Maybe she just likes colors on her nails, hidden away in her shoes, while painting her fingernails black, where people can see?

My frown feels too heavy, and I grind a palm across my brow before pouring some whiskey into a second glass.

"If you must know, I caught myself acting too familiar for our agreed terms of a no-strings, one-night stand, and I was reaffirming a boundary, so nobody gets hurt."

So I don't get hurt, an echo mutters in my head, because I'm having some fucking feelings about this woman, which is something I'm used to hiding from myself, but it feels dangerously close to the surface tonight.

Shelby looks me over and takes one glass of whiskey from the counter. She sips at it and makes a cute face when she swallows, clearly feeling the burn. "Well, okay then." She wets her lips and looks up at me with eyes that are far too trusting. "Shall we commence with the spanking?"

The corner of her mouth twitches, like she's trying to keep her smirk in check, and a low, hungry rumble emanates from deep in my throat. "You like me making your ass hot and bothered, huh?" I say. "Tell me why. Are you feeling needy for discipline? Or is it the reward of the next orgasm you seek?"

She lifts one shoulder. "Maybe I don't care if your

touch comes with a positive or negative charge, as long as you're giving me your full attention."

Her words give me pause, and I set my whiskey back on the counter before leaning against it. "Come here, little miss."

Shelby closes her eyes, and her lashes flutter against her cheeks. She smiles and lifts her nose as if smelling something good, and then a subtle tremor runs through her.

"I like it when you call me that," she says, opening her eyes and stepping closer.

"I noticed." I tug her into me and look down into her pretty eyes, while I sweep her soft, dark hair back from her face. "Has nobody been taking care of you, beautiful? Is that why you came to find me?"

She presses her lips together and squeezes her eyes shut. "I don't... Can we just...?" Her chin quivers, and she firms her jaw, making it still once more. "Will you please take care of me tonight?" she whispers eventually, melting my fucking heart.

She's got two fucking dads but no daddy?

Well, one now, I remember her saying. Loss is her daily ritual. Her family's probably a mess. I know mine is after we lose someone.

I kiss her forehead and scoop her into my arms. "Of course I'll take care of you, pretty darling."

5

JEM

We're back on his bed, and Gunnar's being so sweet and gentle with me.

I hate it.

I liked it before, when he bossed me around and had me do hot, naughty things that made me feel young and fun. Now I feel fragile and pathetic, like I'm too sensitive to plunder or that I require special treatment to keep from breaking. He doesn't seem to realize I felt broken before we met, and I just want him to pound at the pieces a bit, so some will stick back together.

I set myself one task, and that was to get some dick. If I go home a technical *P in V* virgin after having this man lick me out while he thumb-fucked my ass, I'm going to be so fucking disappointed in myself. Self-esteem is built by achieving your goals, and after having all my life plans stripped away, I need some fucking self-esteem, *damn it*.

Every time he whispers Shelby's name, I want to shake my head and tell him to call me *Jem*, but I don't really want to be that sexless girl, tonight, either. I want some new version of me.

He peeled his T-shirt off me and has kissed about every inch of skin I have, but he's barely scuffed me with his beard, and he's so restrained, I can feel the tension in his body growing the more he holds back.

He flicks his tongue at my neck and tugs at my ear for a second, ramping up my hope for something more, but then he trails tiny, delicate kisses down my throat, like I'm a precious little princess. Princess *Shelby*.

The name whispers over my skin again with such reverence, I can't take it. I asked him to take care of me, but I don't want this.

I clamp my hand around his jaw and hold his face, so he'll meet my gaze. "I don't want to be Shelby anymore. Call me *Little Miss* and kiss me like you did before — like you're hungry and don't want to stop. I want you to fuck me. As many times as you want. Make me take your big cock, and then tell me I'm a good girl."

"Anything else?" he asks, a look of intense concentration on his face as he searches mine.

I release my grip on his bearded jaw and stroke the underside of his chin. "Yes."

He raises his eyebrows, apparently waiting for me to expand further.

"I'll also answer to *baby girl*, but I want you to use me like a dirty slut." I press my lips together and study him closely as soon as the words leave my mouth.

Gunnar's lips twitch. "Are you sure about that, Little Miss?"

I nod. "All night. Like you promised. Even if I fall

asleep. Do everything to me. I want to wake up and feel where you've been. I want to feel it for days."

His hand instantly firms on my thigh, and he yanks my legs apart, watching me like a hawk when I gasp.

My heart races, and my nipples grow so tight it's like the temperature suddenly dropped to snap-freeze them hard and pointy.

Gunnar grunts softly. "There's the pretty girl who knows what she wants and isn't afraid to demand it." He smiles and dips his head, to suckle at one of my achingly needy nipples, and I just about push off the bed to get further into his mouth.

What the fuck is he doing with his tongue? It's like he's tugging hard and flicking at me with hot, wet...

"Welcome back, Little Miss," he rumbles, scuffing his bearded chin over my sensitive skin.

I grab his hair and pull him back toward my breast until his lips brush against my nipple. "*Please.*"

He nips at me and suckles so hard I arch off the bed to be able to take the intensity. It almost-hurts, in a good way, and my body doesn't know how it's meant to feel — like when he slapped my ass. It stung, but it made me hot and needy and achy for more.

Gunnar rumbles into my breast, as he tugs at me, and his hard cock keeps thrusting at my lower thigh, making me wish he'd lunge higher and push inside. He's slicking my leg with something wet, and I like the way it feels. I had no idea men also got wet when they were turned on.

He releases my nipple, only to latch onto the other one even more fiercely, and when I cry out and buck my hips at his abs, it spurs him on.

Everything he does shows me that he wants me. His energy, his obvious, escalating need to get closer, and the urgency in his every move almost make me high. How powerful and significant must I be, to have this grown-ass man want me so badly?

That he could be this hungry for my body, makes me feel more than special, and it's a whole new experience. It's filling some sort of appreciation quota for my existence that's been long-neglected, and I'm desperate for more. I want him to fill every gap in my soul I've gained through loss or sacrifice. I want to believe I'm special. I want to be *wanted*.

I spread myself wider, offering him everything. He's so focused on making me feel good, and his every touch is promising something even better.

Gunnar digs his big fingers into my flesh and strains against me with a groan. The strong suction on my nipple eases, and he licks at it as it slips from his mouth. He leans back, and I follow his gaze, admiring his handiwork as I stare at my enlarged, rouged nipples. The sight pleases us both, I think, because he's shamelessly rutting his wetness along my thigh. When he meets my gaze with dilated pupils, he's breathing heavy, and I can tell he's driven himself half-wild with need.

"So fucking pretty, Little Miss. Are you a good girl? Keep yourself clean? Don't let any nasty cock in this sweet, juicy little cunt?" He rubs at my clit until I'm panting, and then pushes his fingers inside me, stretching my inner walls so gloriously that I lift my tail to fuck at his hand.

"I'm a good girl," I utter, whimpering when he stretches me even more.

"You sure are, beautiful. Look at you, wet as fuck for me, taking four fingers in this tiny cunt, like a good, needy little slut. You're so fucking tight, but you're going to take all of me. Aren't you, baby girl? Going to take me in and squeeze me so right. I'm going to love it inside you."

He pulls his hand away, to leave me empty, then drags his body over mine until I feel his thick cock pressing hot against my inner thigh. "I want to push inside your gushing fucking hole right now. Fuck you bare and leave you dripping."

His words make me buck, and the bulbous head of his cock slots between my folds. He moans long and hard, his arms trembling as he holds himself still. "I want to do it, so don't fucking push me, Little Miss," he growls, nudging inward just a little, to stretch my entrance in a forceful tease that makes me rock my hips at him again.

My pelvic thrust wedges him deeper, and he swears out loud before shoving his massive cock hard into me, until I'm so stretched I can barely breathe.

"This what you wanted, Little Miss?" he growls, pumping in and out of me, shoving deeper each time. I take every thick inch of him and cry out in relief. It feels so good to be this full that I could come with just a hint of pressure on my clit. "You want this fat cock to fuck you bare?"

My pussy clamps around him, and he hisses, dragging his cock back and forth through the constriction, and then slamming at me hard before pulling out and leaving me desperate and empty.

He flips me over and slaps my ass three times in quick succession. "No. Fucking. Strings," he rumbles. He climbs off the bed, opens his bedside drawer, and rummages through it, before slamming it shut and hunting through the next one.

My ass stinging in the hottest way, I watch through my hair as he tosses a box of condoms on the nightstand and tears a foil wrapper open with his teeth.

He sheaths his shining cock in seconds, and then strokes it as he looks at me. "Ass in the air, Little Miss. I'm going to spank your greedy little cunt before I fuck it hard."

I do as I'm told, and quickly. There's no denying that I want it. He had me so close to coming after only a few strokes, that I can't wait for him to finish the job.

Now that I've felt his size and warmth inside me, I'm nervous to have him behind me, but the quiver in my thighs has nothing to do with nerves. It's from pure need.

His spanks make me feel things beneath the superficial sting that I can't even describe, but I crave more of it. More of his touch, his firm words, his authority. Some fucking boundaries nobody else cares enough to give me.

I was so carried away with feeling good, I totally would have fucked him bare, but he's stepped into the role of *responsible adult*, and it's like he actually cares what choices I make. I don't have to look after anyone or be the reliable person here.

Comfortable under his mindful supervision, I lift my ass higher, welcoming his approach.

If he's in charge, I don't have to think. Only feel. And I believe his promise to make me feel good.

He rids himself of his jeans completely and climbs onto the bed behind me. I rock back and forth, needy and greedy for cock, like he accused, but he makes me wait for his touch. Part of me is hoping he'll shove his cock into me when I least expect it, and the rest just wants him inside as soon as possible.

"Gunnar?" It feels weird to call him by his name when he never uses mine.

He grips my ass cheeks with his huge hands and spreads them until I feel so open I could tear. The flat of his tongue parts my pussy lips and then the tip flicks at my asshole. I thrust my face into his pillows and squeal-moan from both surprise and pleasure.

The needy squawk gives away my appreciation, and I involuntarily grip the bedding in my fists, tilting my hips to give him even better access. He grunts softly and presses the flat of his thumb to my ass, teasing me by alternating between a sensation of pressure and fast little rubbing motions. Why the fuck do I like it so much? It should feel dirty and wrong. I start to pull away, but Gunnar grips me tightly and holds me in place.

"*Take* the fucking pleasure I give you. Don't run from it. I love watching you get wet from a little ass play, sugar."

He keeps me in place, until I stay on my own, accepting all the attention and feeling grateful for it.

"That's my good girl," he coos. "Relax and open right up. Let's get you good and ready for me. I like that."

I want to call out his name and beg for his cock to fill the throbbing ache in my core, but it doesn't taste right on my tongue when I try to say it. It comes out more like a grumpy little whine.

Gunnar spanks my butt, right over my asshole, where he's been making me all sensitive and wanton. "Don't fret. Just tell me what's on your mind, baby girl."

"I want a play name, to call you," I whisper as he rubs his flat hand in a small circular motion over the heat of his spanking. My asshole is practically vibrating from it, adding a new sensation to the heady mix he's been giving me.

"*Daddy*," he says in a strained whisper. "Call me *Daddy*, and beg for my cock, Little Miss."

I try to do as I'm told, but he's dragging his fingertips up the back of my thigh like claws, and it's new and different, and when he pinches my clit, I shake my head, because I need something else. "Spank me, Daddy. Spank my wet pussy."

The sting hits me, and the impact sends me forward into the pillows with a moan.

Gunnar's beard grazes my upper thighs, and he laps at my pussy like a hungry beast, muttering filthy praise about how pretty and pink I look. He rears back and spanks me again, sending a blast of sensation through my clit this time.

I cry out and grip the pillows. "*Again, Daddy.*"

He rumbles in a scolding tone and rubs at my clit, lightly, evasively, until I beg. "*Please.*"

The slap sets my pussy thrumming, and Gunnar doesn't let up. He spanks me again — a juicy-sounding smack that leaves my thighs spattered in arousal.

"Can you hear how fucking wet you're getting for

Daddy? Getting this tight young cunt ready for a big fucking man. Aren't you, baby girl? Ready, like a good little whore."

My clit takes another sharp slap, and my core clamps hard around nothing. Gunnar grunts, grips my hips roughly, and shoves himself inside me, growling as he forces the bulbous head of his thick cock through my clenched pussy. He forges deep, and moans as I pant and squirm to adjust to the stretch.

"Such a good, tight girl." He thrusts into me again and again, forcing his way in, and then sliding back out with more ease. "Little miss... fucking perfect," he mumbles. He sinks deep and strums my needy clit with one hand, as he holds himself seated to the hilt.

He runs his other hand up and down my back, slaps my ass, and then slides his hand to my underside, to cup the softness of my lower belly. "If things were different, I'd sow fucking oats in here any day of the fucking week, just to watch them grow."

My core flutters, and he hums softly, as his cock jerks inside me. He grinds my clit into his fingers and reaches up to squeeze my jostling breasts and tweak a nipple hard enough to make me hiss.

"You're going to be a breeder one day. Aren't you, baby girl?" he rumbles, sliding his fat cock back and forth slowly. "Going to make some daddy a happy man. Round belly. Baby on your tit."

His movements pick up speed and strength, and it's all I can do, to hang on to the pillows as he pounds me. He angles me into his hand, forcing pleasure to ripple through me from clit to core, until I'm pulled so tight around his massive cock, he feels like a giant.

"Going to let Daddy suck on your tits, too," he says, fucking me hard enough to set my breasts swinging. "Let him fuck you every day. Keep your pretty little cunt full of seed."

All I can imagine is what he says, and I buck backward into him, wanting every part of it without fully understanding why. My head is spinning in a whirling mess of filthy words, and my body's so high on sensation I could explode any second.

This is exactly what I wanted. A night of pleasure — an absolute difference to my everyday. He's even giving me an imagined future of family bliss I can escape into.

"Daddy's going to fill me up," I agree, lost in the power of his thrusts, as he drives me closer to climax. "Make me take his cock all the time."

"I will," he rumbles. "I'll even fuck you while you sleep."

"*Yes. Daddy.*" I cry out, and my pussy starts to quiver on the edge of orgasm.

Gunnar shoves his cock deep and groans as he rubs my clit hard and fast.

"You'll wake up with cock inside you every morning," he grinds out between his teeth, while I tremble beneath his huge, powerful body. "No fucking panties allowed. Isn't that right, Little Miss?" His husky whisper rasps near my ear, and his rough beard drags against my shoulder.

He tilts me into his rubbing fingers just a little more, and the tiny shift makes a massive difference. The tingling in my clit rushes into a zinging blast that has me moaning an octave higher, when my entire body lights up with the pleasure.

"Easy access, all the time. For Daddy's... big... *cock*," he roars, punctuating each word with a hard thrust, to shove me over the edge.

I explode around him, thrashing and wailing and contracting, as he keeps me full of cock and feelings.

He drives hard at my limits and tenses, muttering about what a good fucking girl I am between grunted moans.

And I feel *deserving* of the praise. I'm his good girl, coming around his big cock so hard I can't stop.

"*Daddy*," I wail, feeling every part of me collapsing.

"I've got you, baby girl," he whispers, and guides us sideways, so he can keep stoking little quivers of pleasure from my limp, spent body.

I feel so perfectly used, but in a way that fills my soul instead of depleting it. "Thank you," I whisper, as I fall into a heavy, sleepy, drunken-like state.

"I'm not done taking care of you," he breathes against my neck, making me shiver. "But rest a little, for now. Daddy's got you."

6

GUNNAR

I've fucked her twice, and she rides like a dream. I can't get enough. My dick's still inside her from the last time.

And I'm hard again.

Her back shivers against my front, and my eyes snap open, as I feel the subtle pleasure tremor ripple through her body to tease my cock. No longer dozing, I rock my hips back and forth, gently fucking her tight cunt while she's sleeping.

Shelby's gorgeous body is fucking spent, but I can't get enough.

This girl doesn't say no. Despite the fucking poundings I gave her tiny little cunt, she kept opening her legs and asking for more. She loves her tits being sucked and her ass being played with, and she appreciates a rough fuck from a big man far more than someone her size should. She's literally given herself to me for the night, trusting I'll do right by her.

And I will.

She's come four times already, and her little cunt was so fucking swollen from our first fuck, that I shoved ice cubes inside her and gave her pain relief before indulging her with sweet treats and gentle hands to help her recover. I don't think I've ever had a woman nearly come just from being massaged, but she's so fucking responsive to a little TLC, I have to wonder what the fuck *is* happening in her life.

Whatever it is, I'm pretty sure I helped her forget about it for a while.

I doubt she's had much experience with men, but she's been enthusiastic as hell. Like she had a bingo card of sexual shenanigans she was on a mission to check off, and her open-mindedness turned me on as much as the rest of her. The more we played, the more compatible we felt. She trusted me with her body, and I fucking loved the opportunity to give her everything she needed.

Even the aftercare made me tingle, inside and out.

All I did was give a shit about her. I cared for her tiring body, while she gazed up at me with grateful eyes, like she hasn't known kindness in too long. I'm so fucking curious about her, and I asked a lot of questions, but she only gave me vague information because... *no strings*.

No strings means no connection beyond this encounter, and she's adamant about sticking to that agreement. But I keep thinking about our bodies tangled together with enough string to bind us with permanent knots, and it makes my heart feel light and floaty.

I know she's young and smart and troubled, and I'm just some filthy old asshole with a history of commitment issues, but I like her, and this night has been unbelievably easy and joyful, in a way I've never encountered before, and I don't want it to end. I'm going to risk asking her out on a date before we say *goodbye* in the morning. *Fuck*, I'll ask her to breakfast and see if she'll reconsider the whole no-strings issue.

I smile to myself and kiss the back of her head, as I slide my cock deeper inside her. I feel amazingly hot and snug in her tight little cunt, and when I give her a few leisurely thrusts, there's an easy glide, like she's still fucking juicy. My cock feels slick as hell. I should change the condom from our last fuck, but I like the illusion the wetness it's giving me.

I utter a soft moan, as I fuck in and out of her limp little body, imagining myself bare inside her. Her cunt is barely big enough to hold me, and I could fill her with cum so easily. I run my hand over her big tits, and then cup her soft belly.

What if I quit my fucking around and gave myself a chance with this sweet girl? What if I flooded her with seed and nurtured her as she grew round and full with it?

My cock strains inside her, excited by the thought.

She'd make beautiful babies — sparkling eyes, clear skin, and cheeky smiles.

Shelby moans softly and shifts her ass against me in her sleep, taking my cock deeper and making me shudder with delight.

I need to get rid of this condom. There's no way it'll handle two loads, and I'm too wired and randy to sleep now. I want to come again.

"Daddy needs to tend the chores," I whisper against Shelby's shoulder before kissing her soft skin. She shivers and murmurs in her sleep, and her pussy tries to snag me, so I can't retreat. "I'll be back inside you soon, baby girl, I promise." Not bothering to hide my grin, I hold the rubber to the base of my cock and slowly pull out, loving the feel of the glide.

But my pleasure is short lived, when I realize the condom fucking broke inside her. That's why it felt so fucking good the last time I came. Why it felt so good inside her, only moments ago. I was fucking *bare* in there.

Panic and curiosity war with each other, and I look at Shelby's sweet, blissfully unaware, sleeping face.

"Oh, Little Miss, we've had an *oops*. An... inappropriately exciting and cock-plumping, but complicating little *oops*," I say softly to her still snoozing form, as I run my hand up and down her thigh.

She's so tired, curled up all naked and pretty. She barely rouses beyond shifting into my touch.

This news is going to ruin her rest, and I'm reluctant to end such a perfectly uplifting night with a drama we can't deal with until the morning anyway. She'll be properly awake then, and I'll be ready to support her however she needs it when I tell her what happened.

Fucking condoms.

I tug the shreds from my hard dick, staring at the pretty shine she's left on me. That *we've* left. It's *our* shine. I fucking came inside her.

My veiny cock swells again at the thought, and I gaze at Shelby's bare ass, which I was snuggled against mere moments ago. With eyes on her sleeping face, I ease myself down the bed, to move in close. Then I spread her ass cheeks and pussy lips, so I can see her seeded cunt.

The sight of my cum, leaking out of her, sends a wave of tingles up my spine, and my heart starts to drum harder and faster, like the rising crescendo in a rock song. My breedy little fantasies are coming true, and even though we'll need to talk about how we'll deal with this in the morning, nothing can change the fact that she's full of my sperm, which could be impregnating her. Right now.

She could be making a baby for me.

"That's a pretty, swollen, and creamed cunt, Little Miss. Going to make a baby for Daddy?" I whisper, licking her cum-soaked pussy while I fuck my hand. "I'll take good care of you both, until we make the next one."

She's on her side, and I guide her top leg to move higher, to see my seed spilling out of her, but what this maneuver really does, is give me better access.

My blood rushes in my veins, and a feverish need comes over me. I shouldn't do it, but she told me to stay inside her before she fell asleep. She *told* me I could fuck her in the night if I felt the need.

And I am *definitely* feeling the fucking need.

It was an accident, but I've already come inside her, and the thought of doing it again is getting me over-whelmingly hot.

With no reason to use a condom now, I climb over her and push inside her wet little cunt, the way I want to.

She moans as I force my way through her tightness, and she lifts her hindquarters a little, inviting me deeper before she settles back into her sleepy daze.

If she wakes up properly, I'll make her come and explain what's happened, but I'm kind of hoping she'll stay asleep a while so we don't have to have that talk. I'm too in love with the idea of breeding her, and I want to enjoy that fantasy before reality puts an end to my playtime.

To keep from disturbing her too much, I take it slow and fuck her nice and gentle.

I'm fucking stealth-breeding her, which feels twice as fucking naughty and exciting, and I want to make it last, but I'm so fucking turned on, I don't know if I can.

She's soaked with our combined juices, and her cunt slurps and squelches with my every move. It's driving me crazy. I want to spill into her again, until she's such a mess, there's no way she'll walk away from me without my seed dripping down her thighs.

I fuck her fast, feeling every hot, slippery groove inside her rub along my shaft, setting my knob alight with sensation. I watch my big, wet cock pumping in and out of her stretched little fuck-hole and feel like a villain. Like I'm fucking away her innocence and making her mine. *Mine.*

My orgasm tears through me, spurting into her depths in brutal jets of pleasure. Right down deep inside her, at the entrance to her womb. I empty my fucking soul into her, nudging it closer to hers, so they can join and spark a new life.

Her pussy ripples around me, as if her body's accepting the gift, and I give her a firm and final thrust. She whimpers softly. Stirs and rocks her ass a little. Clamps at my cock with gentle, quivering spasms, before settling into a deeper sleep with a satisfied sigh.

Light-headed and high from creaming her while she sleeps, I gaze down at her, utterly enamored. "Well done,

Little Miss," I whisper, patting her on the ass. "Taking Daddy's cum twice, like a sweet, fertile girl."

I slip from her cunt and watch my seed trickle out of her. I smear it over her ass and thighs, to see her shine with it, and then I force myself to clean her up a bit before settling in behind her for some rest.

It's not long before I'm getting hard again, because I can't stop thinking about how much I've enjoyed myself with her. Tomorrow could hold any number of possibilities, but I'll have to wait and see where things go once I've told her about the split condom, reassured her that I'm clean, and explained there's a chance she may get pregnant. We'll talk about how best to move forward from that, and I'll support her in whatever she wants.

She'll probably want the Plan-B pill, and I'll take her to the pharmacy and get it for her. But is there a chance she'll want to wait and see what happens? Could I convince her to keep our baby if we made one?

God, I hope she'll let me take her for breakfast before I drive her home. I want to know her better, and I definitely want her tight young cunt tugging cum from my cock again, while she begs for me to suck her tits and mark her pretty skin with my teeth. She's so fucking cute.

My dick strains against her ass, and I hug her close, pushing back inside her swollen and restrictive, cum-slicked pussy with a sigh of relief. She feels like home, and I nuzzle into her hair when she shivers and moans.

"Sleep well, Little Missy," I whisper. "Daddy's got you."

I don't know what tomorrow morning will bring, but I

have loved every second of our time together, and I'm going to do whatever it takes, to get more.

I ROLL over and stretch my heavy limbs with a groan. I need way more sleep.

I drained my tanks to zero last night, for a beautiful young woman who needed my full fucking attention. "And I was glad to give you my all," I mumble with a smile, as I roll back to snuggle in behind her again.

My searching hand finds nothing but empty bed, and I snap my eyes open. "Shelby?"

I throw back the covers, to stare at the space where she'd been, but the thick smell of sex and my sad, lonely cock are the only traces of her left.

A mad, rushing check confirms my house is empty. I even run upstairs, to check the rooms up there, but she's gone, and my heart won't quit pounding so loud I can't think.

When? *How?*

My truck is in the driveway, but I wish she'd stolen it, so I could call the police and get help to track her down, because I have no idea where to look for her, and...

A cold, sweaty dread falls over me, and I groan. I run my hands through my hair and tug it into a sharp, stinging grip.

The broken condom.

I fucked her bare. *Twice.* She won't know what happened, but she definitely needs to. I've *got* to fucking find her.

Where to start?

I rush back to my room, pull on last night's jeans, and hunt around the floor for my T-shirt. I look everywhere, but it's not here, either. Does Shelby have it? *God*, she looked so fucking cute in it last night.

I hope she is wearing it now. Is that weird? For her to do that? For me to want it? Am I hoping I made such an impression, she needed a fucking souvenir?

A string of cuss words leaves my mouth, and I grab a new T-shirt from the drawer and pull it on as I head out front, to grab my keys. I need to track her down.

How long ago did she leave? She can't be far. There's no bus route, and a cab ride back to town would be crazy-expensive, not to mention it'd take time for the taxi to get here. Maybe she left on foot, and I can catch up.

On *foot*? Was she fucking *running* from me?

The terrible gnawing sensation in my gut makes me wind down the window a bit, for some fresh air, as I head down the mountain.

Did she leave without saying *goodbye* because I scared her? I was too rough? She didn't like my commanding, possessive behavior?

My dick wakes up with an opinion, and I shake my head. She definitely liked it. She fucking begged for me to fuck her harder, at one point.

I look each way at the intersection. There's not a single soul in sight, and it's the first time in my life that I've fucking hated it. With a loud moan, I rest my head on the steering wheel.

I'm a country boy, born and raised, and I like nothing better than getting away from it all, but I wish with all my might that I could see Shelby's pretty, round ass swinging its way toward town. Instead, I get nothing but empty fields and trees and fresh air.

I sit at the intersection. Would she even know which way to go? I'm pretty sure she was as distracted as I was when we paused here last night — when she fucked her fingers all juicy and made me fall in love with her cute, perverted little hobbies and her use of big words and her soft, needy gasps.

It's harder to breathe, all of a sudden, and I wind my window down all the way, so the breeze can push into my lungs while I drive onward to town.

I didn't fall in love with a virtual stranger like an idiot. I didn't. I can't be that fucking predictable, passing up every offer of love for years, and then *losing* the one woman I finally connect with.

It was a no-strings-attached agreement. I knew that, going in. And the more I think about trying to play house with such a clever and pretty young woman, the older, stupider, and more pathetic I feel. What in the world would she want with me?

Get *real*, Gunnar Scott.

I'm not desperately trying to find her so I can forge a binding connection; I just need to do right by her and explain what happened, so there really are no strings. That's what she asked for, and that's what I said I'd provide.

It doesn't matter that she's the most honest woman I've ever met or that our chemistry was off the charts.

I'm not really daddy-material. I'm more of a lone

wolf. The kind of catch who should be tossed back, before I do unexpected and permanent damage.

Above all, I'm a seasoned adult, and she's barely grown. I will act responsibly. I'll make sure she's okay, and then I'll leave her be and sort out my fucking daddy issues on my own, because I definitely fucking have some.

So...

Where could she be? What do I even really know about her?

———

THERE ARE three department stores in town.

Two of them employ someone named *Shelby*.

Only one of those is a woman.

And she isn't *my* Shelby.

She has a similar shade of hair, and her eyes are blue, and she's young and quite pretty, but she's not my *Little Miss*.

After a few moments of staring at her in disappointment, I shake my head. "Sorry. I'm looking for a different Shelby. There isn't another one working here?" I say, hopeful as fuck.

She purses her lips and shrugs. "Far as I know, I'm the only Shelby in town."

"Actually, there's a guy over at the Metrotown Plaza electronic store with the same name," I say with a sad smile. "Thanks anyway. Sorry to have bothered you."

"No bother, handsome." She flashes me a bright smile, and I practically shudder at the thought of her getting flirty with me, even though she's pretty and seems nice.

Normally, I'd follow that shit up with some smooth talking, until she let me fuck her in a back room, but that thought is literally repellent right now. How fucked up am I after one night of bare fucking? How fast does a breeding kink even develop? I'm so messed up.

"Have a nice day, then," I mumble, walking away faster than is polite.

I can't find my girl, and it kind of feels like my heart is breaking.

My girl?

My body responds in full favor to the notion. *My girl.* The woman I came inside, while I fantasized about claiming her as mine. The one who left before I woke.

She got away clean, which was what she wanted, I guess. She could probably sense I wasn't worth investing in, right off the bat. Good for a fuck, but not fucking good enough for anything else.

She wouldn't be wrong to think so. Worn out from playing the provider when I was young, I trained myself to be the unavailable guy. Happy to play the role of cool uncle, but not dad. I didn't want to be a real father. Those guys only fuck you up.

I sigh, check the time, and head back out to the mountain, to help get my sister's kids where they need to go. Her husband hasn't been able to drive since his accident, and she's been run off her feet. They can use all the help they can get, and lucky for them, I've got time to spare, because I've spent my adult life making sure nobody else needs me. Forty-two and alone.

What a shitty fucking legacy.

And I'm fantasizing about breeding a college-aged girl.

What part of my sick, twisted little brain thinks I'm father material?

I'd better fucking swear off love and women until I get my stupid head straight.

7

JEM

THE NEXT YEAR...

I snap my bubblegum, jiggle Viv on my shoulder, and add an extra pack of diapers to my cart — the next size up, because she's growing so fast she'll probably need them by the time we finish the first pack. Her daddy was a pretty big guy, so maybe she'll take after him.

"Excuse me, miss? Your little Cinderella dropped her slipper."

I turn at the man's voice, and my bubblegum just about falls from my mouth when my jaw drops open.

Gunnar Scott is holding out one of Viv's booties.

He freezes too, and we stare at each other, both apparently speechless.

He drops his gaze to Viv, and his eyes widen as fast as my face flushes with heat.

When he lifts his eyes to meet mine, I open my mouth to say something — anything — but no words come out. He's frowning, and he looks like he has about a hundred questions. As well he might.

I don't know what he'll ask first when he seems about to speak, only that I want him not to be mad at me. My eyes tear up in a heartbeat, and his face softens instantly.

"*Shelby*." He says it so softly, so sweetly — he can see how fragile I am.

I shake my head. "*Jem*," I correct him, before my voice cracks.

His complexion pales. "You gave me a fake name?"

I nod and sniff back my threatening tears. "I'm sorry. I... I can explain."

"You wanted no strings." He stares at Viv again, and I can see him doing the fucking math. "I tried to track you down after you left," he says, "but you... didn't want to be found. And now...?"

Suddenly, I want to be anywhere but the fucking grocery store, and Viv's starting to suck on my shoulder, hungry again, like always. I chew my gum hard and fast, looking around for somewhere to take her, but the car is probably the best place. More than ready to abandon my cart before she screams the place down, I take a step back, but my balance takes an unapproved vacation thanks to my trembling legs, and all I do is wobble on the spot.

Gunnar reaches out to steady us. "Are you okay?"

I nod, but then shake my head. "I need to go sit in my car."

Gunnar looks between our shopping carts — mine filled with diapers, and his filled with baking supplies and beer. He moves them both to one side of the aisle and nods. "Okay. Let's go," he says, like there's no option other than his coming with me.

There isn't, I guess. I have some explaining to do.

He escorts me to my car and helps settle Viv and me into the passenger seat, like a gentleman. A strong, supportive gentleman, who smells unbelievably good up close, like he did when we met.

It's so easy to close my eyes and remember exactly what it felt like to have his big arms keeping me safe and secure. While he fucked me like he'd die if he didn't. While he made me come, and then made me a mom.

Viv begins to fuss, and I swear under my breath, rushing to get my breast out for her. "Sorry. If I don't get her latched on fast, there'll be hell to pay. The girl knows what she wants, and she's a bit of a screamer."

I get her positioned, and relax when she begins suckling.

Gunnar crouches at my feet, eyes brimming with all the questions he must have.

"Jem?" He looks me over and swallows visibly, and then stares at Viv's little cheeks while she's chugging milk, like he's obsessed over her getting enough nutrition. "Am I...?"

I run my fingers over Viv's soft, blonde curls and try not to look at Gunnar's short and slightly darker curls as I straighten her little bow with a sigh. "So... maybe there weren't exactly *no* strings," I admit in a quiet voice.

"She's mine?" he asks in a whisper, taking a seat right on the ground of the parking lot, like he needs dirt and old gum on his jeans. "A—are you sure?"

"Positive," I reply without hesitation. "I haven't been with another man." I watch him closely before adding, "Ever."

He draws his eyebrows downward, and then he sits

up straight and stares at me. "What do you mean? You were —" He covers his mouth as a strangled noise escapes his throat. "A virgin?" he whispers, looking absolutely horrified. "And you let me...?"

He launches off the ground and paces in front of me.

8

GUNNAR

Oh, my fucking *God*.

I want to throw myself in front of the next passing car.

I fucked her like an animal. A sweet little virgin. Who lied about who she was and...

"Why did you lie to me about that? About anything? Shelby, I..."

Not Shelby. "*Jem*."

No wonder I couldn't fucking find her.

I drop my gaze to the baby girl at her breast — *my* baby girl. I have a fucking daughter and a young mom to take care of, and I can't take my eyes off either one of them.

My dick fucking loves the sight of my long-lost Little Miss feeding our baby at her breast. No bottles. Just skin contact, pure love, and a kind of comfort that our little girl clearly fucking appreciates. The baby's guzzling down the milk like she can't get enough.

She's so fucking cute. Little blonde curls, chubby

cheeks, and big blue eyes, not too dissimilar to her mother's.

This tiny little miracle is part me, too.

The thought hits me with an intensity I wasn't expecting, and moments from my night with Jem flash through my mind, making me want to reach out and touch the evidence of what we did. What *I* did.

I haven't been able to get this woman out of my head for nearly a year, and now she's holding my baby.

I fucked her bare, knocked her up, and she *kept* the baby. I'm a father. And it's all wrong. This isn't what I wanted at all.

I'm an absentee father.

The worst kind of father there is.

I would never do that to my woman and child if I knew. But how could I know when Jem hid the truth so well?

I missed everything. Missed getting to know Jem. Missed watching her fertile little body grow beautifully round with my seed. Missed helping her when she needed support. Missed caring for her and my baby, leaving her to go through everything all alone — like a fucking asshole. I didn't even get a chance to celebrate any of it with her.

Did she celebrate? Or does she hate me?

Was she scared? Is that why she didn't tell me?

She's so young, and a baby is such a big, life-changing thing. Did she think I would be mad if I found out? Because of the lies she told me when we met? Was her family mad? There's so much I don't know. Why didn't she tell me? And why did she feel she had to lie about who she was? She was out to get laid... Did she think I wouldn't fuck her if I knew the truth? Why would she need to lie about her identity in the bar that night?

My racing thoughts spin and scramble, while the blood rushes in my ears, and then everything goes silent, as the cogs click into place on something so ominous, I want to throw up just thinking about it. "How old are you really?"

"Almost nineteen," she squeaks.

I sink to my knees on the ground in front of her and lower my head to my hands with a groan. "You're just a *kid*? What the fuck were you doing in a bar, drinking? You had ID. It was... fake," I mutter to myself, squeezing my eyes shut, as the urge to puke turns my stomach.

I recall her flashing a driver's license at the bar staff, and then declaring herself old enough to take dick. "Why would you...?" I ask her. "Was it a dare? See who could score the oldest guy? Did you win? I'm forty-fucking-*three*. I... *Oh God,* I'm *more* than twice your age. Double was bad enough, but this is unforgivable. I'm a fucking *pedo*?"

My stomach's empty, but I dry-heave at her feet, like the sick fuck I am, because I fucking loved every second my cock was in this young woman, and watching her feed my baby was giving my dick the fun-tingles literally moments ago. "I want to kick my ass so fucking hard right now," I say with a groan. "Why didn't you *tell* me?" I growl, staying low as I gaze up at her, so I don't seem like a huge, daunting beast.

Jem stops chewing and tightens her jaw. "I wanted

you to fuck me, and I was old enough to ask, so I did. You didn't do anything wrong."

I groan again and bend my head to her car door for stability. "I did. I fucking did. The condom broke, and I was going to tell you when you woke up, but I couldn't find you anywhere," I explain. "I looked, Little Miss. I found two Shelbys, at two department stores, but neither of them was you, and that was the only information I had to go on. I fucking drove the streets, searching for your face, but you weren't out there."

"I'm kind of a homebody and don't get out much." She shrugs. "And a broken condom makes a lot of sense, now that you say it, but unless you tore it open on purpose, my getting pregnant wasn't your intention, so you don't need to beat yourself up about it."

What's done is done, and she's clearly adjusted to it, but she's being too fucking kind. She needs to know the truth.

I sack up and meet her gaze. "It's definitely my fault," I confess. "Once I realized the condom was broken and you were full of cum, there was no point holding back when I wanted to come inside you again."

Jem sits a little straighter, and the baby slips off her tit. Her nipple is so much thicker and darker than I remember, and the sight of a pale droplet forming on the tip before she gets the baby latched back on makes my dick take a lot more notice.

"You came inside me on purpose?" she asks, her voice strained.

I nod and wait for her to cuss me out, but her face isn't angry.

Her lips are parted, her cheeks are flushed, and her eyes look almost hopeful, for some reason. She looks almost excited that I filled her little cunt with spunk, and I stammer. "I... The damage was done, and you'd fallen asleep with my cock inside you, and you felt so fucking good. Knowing you'd taken my seed inside you, made me crave it even more, and I..."

She shivers, and I swear under my breath. I hold my hand to my chest. "I was going to talk to you about it in the morning, I swear. Take you to get the Plan-B pill, if you wanted it. But you were *gone*. I couldn't find you anywhere, and I didn't know what to think. I thought I scared you. Or hurt you. That maybe you fucking hated me, for doing all those things to you, when you were so sweet, and... Obviously, I'm a despicable fucking *predator*." I scold myself for leaning in, putting a soothing hand on her leg, and wanting to repeat every fucking thing we did. I hurriedly pull my hand away.

"I *asked* you to do those things to me," she says in a cool tone.

"You didn't ask me to fuck a baby into your young, little, virgin body," I growl, hating the way my cock loves every part of that phrase.

I moan as my dick strains in my jeans, and I purposely twist, giving it a burning pinch with the denim, to settle it down.

"If I had asked for that, would you have done it?" she asks, taking me by surprise.

I want to say *no*, but it would sound like the lie it is. "Yes," I whisper instead.

She presses her lips together, nods, and leans back in her seat, to watch the baby nurse again.

"When I found out I was pregnant, I kind of pretended I *did* ask for that," she says quietly, shifting on her ass a bit. "I liked the idea of having your baby a lot. So much so, I decided to keep her, even though I knew you and the rest of the world might look down on me for it."

I open my mouth to reassure her, but she blows a bubble with her gum, and it's a soul-crushing reminder of how inappropriately young she is. What is my sister going to say? I wouldn't even let her date unchaperoned when she was eighteen.

"I've been trying to work up the courage to tell you," she says softly. "I just wanted to have my shit together, so you could see I was self-sufficient and not after anything from you. Believe it or not, this little girl is one of the best things to happen to me. I'm finding success and enjoying motherhood, and I'm happy with my choice to keep our baby, but I didn't think you'd feel the same, and I didn't want you to..." She blinks at me with her big blue eyes, and I want to fucking melt.

"I'm not unhappy to find out I'm a father," I assure her. "A little stunned, maybe, but... who could be mad about this?" I reach out, to touch my baby's curls.

Jem smiles a little as she snorts. "I can think of plenty of people I know who'd be more upset than you are right now. I lied to you, and I broke the one rule we set. We agreed there would be no strings, and I... I chose not to sever this one. I could never be sorry for this little girl, but I am sorry for the way I treated you."

If she knew fluttering her eyelashes at me like this

would make me forgive her almost anything, she wouldn't be as worried.

"You don't owe me any apologies, Jem, I promise you. And while I wish I could have supported you through what must have been a difficult period, I'm glad for the choice you made to keep this little miracle," I say sincerely, looking up at her, and then returning my gaze to our baby. "She's beautiful. Does she have a name?"

"*Viviana Beatrix Wade*," Jem says proudly before blushing. "Viv for short... Do you approve?"

"She's clearly a little Viv," I say with a smile, touching the baby's curls again. "Viviana Beatrix Wade."

It's not as good as Viviana Beatrix *Scott*, but I like it.

"*Viviana* makes her sound pretty and special, and a little badass, too. Not unlike her mother." I sigh as I look over the pretty young woman who made a first impression that lasted me all year and will now last my lifetime. "The name tastes good when it rolls off my tongue. It sort of cries *esteemed, old-world glamor,* but with an *alive and kicking* feel to it. I like it."

Jem's blush deepens. "Thank you."

She fidgets with Viv's booties for a moment, and then looks at me again. "It's good that I ran into you. I've been having the hardest time, finding the energy to cope with more consequences, and I didn't want you to hate me. I didn't want to be something you regretted, because that's an awful thing to think about your child's mother, and I..."

She chews her gum a few times, takes a couple of deep breaths, and keeps her head low, watching me from beneath her dark lashes. "I said *no strings*, and that can still be the deal, Gunnar. I presumed I'd be raising this baby alone when I made the decision to keep her, and I'm not asking you for help. I don't expect anything from you, and I—"

"You think I would father a child and not take responsibility for her?" My tone is harsh, and her head snaps up, like I intended. "I don't abandon my people, Jem," I say firmly. "I take care of them. I'm not letting you do this on your own. This is a whole new human being we're talking about, and Viv's going to take a lot of input. You're going to need help, and I'm going to be here. Helping."

Her dark eyebrows dip in the center, and she opens her mouth to say something, but I shake my head and stand. "I won't miss out on more of my kid's life than I already have."

Her frown deepens. "She's barely two months old. You haven't really missed anything."

"Haven't *missed* anything?" My lips flap without sound, and I push myself up to standing, while I stare at her. "It's been *months*. I didn't get time to adjust. I didn't get to make things easier for you. I have no idea how you're doing — if you've been sick, if you have enough money to live, to be safe and comfortable and well-fed. Who's been taking care of you? Supporting you? Doing the emergency midnight diaper runs so you can rest? Getting you whatever you need, to give Viv the best start? Are you stressed or tired? How was the birth?" I gasp. "Did you suffer?"

My voice cracks, and I cover my mouth. "Did I make you suffer?"

Jem's frown deepens. "Are you serious?"

I squint at her. "What else would I be, given the circumstances? I'm forty-three-years old, and I made you a teenage fucking *mom*. The least I can do is give a fuck and provide you with whatever support you need."

She lifts one of her shoulders slightly, and her breathing is all shallow. She's also gazing up at me like I'm fucking wonderful or some shit.

"I've been fine," she says eventually. "I mean, I was a little nauseous in the beginning, and I've been horny as fuck for months on end without reprieve. Frustratingly, that's only been escalating since I ran into you. You came inside me, and liked it; you're already smitten with Viv; and I didn't think I was the swooning type about this sort of thing, but you just got adorably feisty about being a good provider and an active participant in our lives, like a gorgeous fucking asshole, and now I'm all hot and needy with—"

She cuts herself off and snaps her mouth shut as tightly as her legs. I'm sure my shocked, open-mouthed staring is what gave her pause.

"What the... *fuck*?" The last word wheezes from me, like I'm deflating, because my cock is fucking swelling, and that's so wrong a reaction, I can't even begin to understand it. "Don't do this to me, Little Miss. I need you to hush your pretty fucking mouth before I get you in any more trouble — if that's even fucking possible."

I run my hands through my hair and glance at the supermarket. "I didn't think I was the kind of guy who was into younger women, but you've been confusing the hell out of me since we met, and I need you to not say hot shit like that to me. It makes it hard to think, and my base instincts aren't what I should be following."

I pace back and forth next to her car. "I want to do what's best for everyone here. Right now, that's making sure Viv is taken care of, which means I have to think with my head, not my cock. I'm too old to be the right man for you, Jem, but I'll be the right father for Viv, I swear. I'll be a good dad."

Jem lifts the milk-drunk baby to her shoulder and burps her. "You want to hold her while I put myself back together?" she asks.

"Do I...?" I'm already nodding. "Yes. Please."

She passes Viv to me, and I marvel at our baby a moment before pulling her close and breathing her in. She smells of milky sweetness and baby soap, and my heart can hardly take it. "It's nice to meet you, Viviana Beatrix Wade," I whisper and kiss her on the forehead.

She clenches her fists and starts turning red, scrunching her face, so I rest her against my shoulder, to finish burping her.

"You seem experienced." Jem narrows her eyes at me when Viv gives up some of her air bubbles. "Just how many wild oats have you sown, Gunnar Scott?"

"Viv is my first," I assure her. "But my little sister, Chiara, has four kids, so I've held a few babies. I kind of helped raise her out of diapers, too, so I come with recommendations for the whole *Dad* gig. I mean, you don't know Chiara, so I can't prove it until you've met her, but she's a good girl. My mom said she was proud of the way I cared for them both after Dad left, and even though Mom's no longer here to help, I won't let you down, Jem.

I won't be the guy who pretends to care, and then leaves you. I fucking hate that guy."

"Me too," she says, her eyes getting a little teary.

"Hey, now," I say softly. "You okay?"

She sniffs and avoids my eyes. "Just emotional. Lack of sleep combined with confronting the guy I've been avoiding for months about the baby we made, and him being really fucking sweet and nice about it..." She shrugs and clears her throat. "I'm fine. I... I need to go get my groceries."

I move Viv into the crook of my arm. "You mind if I keep holding her and come with?" I ask as the baby snuggles in. "I can't stop looking at her. She's so fucking cute, Jem. Is that short for *Jemma*?"

She nods, her face flushing bright pink as she holds out her hand to shake mine. "Jemma Wade," she says with a shy smile. "I should have told you. I just didn't want to get kicked out of the bar, and then I didn't want you to turn me down for being too young, when I meant what I said. I was old enough to take dick, Gunnar."

I grunt in agreement. She took my dick well, and quite a few times, as I recall. My softening cock jerks with interest again, and I distract myself by changing the subject as we walk back to the store. "So, tell me about yourself, Jemma Wade. The truth, if you don't mind. I feel incredibly uncomfortable, knowing so little about you. And while we did agree to *no strings* at the time, after the night we spent together, I had every intention of tracking you down, explaining what happened, and asking you out again, so please don't skimp on details. I want to know all the important things — from before and after we last met."

When I fucked a baby into your soft, young, fertile, little belly.

Oh my *God*, I'm going to have to quit thinking about that shit.

I need to be on my best behavior and never touch the poor girl again, because I can only imagine how things are going to go down when I introduce myself to her father.

The grocery store is busier when we return, and we have to start from scratch because our abandoned carts are nowhere to be found.

"Do you want to share a cart, so you can keep holding Viv?" I ask. "I noticed you didn't have that much stuff, anyway."

"Uh... sure," Gunnar replies, barely taking his eyes off Viv.

Besotted is probably the best term to describe him right now. He continually stares at her, touches her cheeks and her hair, straightens her clothes, and adjusts the little bow in her hair.

It's probably a good thing she's so fucking cute. I think it really eased the blow of his finding out he's a dad.

Plus, it sounds like he got pretty excited about coming inside me, and after months of thinking about that night and what must have happened, I have to say, his fucking a baby into me on purpose has been my top fantasy. In that daydream, I usually end up living with him in his cabin in the mountains and having more of his babies, while he makes sure I come morning, noon, and night. In reality, I'm way more independent and untrusting, but I can't help what comes to mind when I think of this man.

"So I like your shirt," he says with a smirk.

My face flares with heat, and I squeeze my eyes shut a moment, before I clear my throat. "Hope you don't mind that I borrowed it." I wince. "I didn't want the Uber guy staring at my tits in that dress."

"*Uber*," he says with a nod. "I fucking wondered how you got away." He looks me over and smiles. "I don't mind you, wearing it. Looks good on you."

My cheeks get even warmer, and I duck my head. "Thanks."

"And how are your frisky, woolly woodland creatures going?" he asks, a smile in his voice.

"Good, actually. I now film them and put the videoclips on TikTok, and I have enough followers to earn a living. Which means I can comfortably stay home with Viv and give her everything she needs."

Gunnar stares at me. "I only understood about half of what you just said. But it was the important half, I think. You make videos of your creatures, and people pay to watch them?"

I snort softly. "You sound like such a boomer. The age-gap thing was really hot until just now." I give him a cheeky grin and pull out my phone to show him one of my clips.

"The vibe is cute little critters, doing sweet, wholesome things, to bring a little joy into people's social-media feeds. Help balance out life's drama factor. The world needs more happiness, and that's what I get out of it, so I thought I'd spread some around."

Gunnar watches and re-watches, captivated, until I swipe another video into view, so he can see some of my other work. I'm quite proud of the nimble fox family, playing frisbee.

"These are frickin' adorable." He returns his gaze to me, as the video starts its loop again. "You're... famous?"

I roll my eyes. "Everyone's famous, Gunnar. I'm one of the many who've learned to monetize a hobby, so I can enjoy my work. Because, if we don't enjoy ourselves, then what's the point. Right? A wise man once told me life's too short, to waste my time on shit that doesn't serve."

The un-bearded apples of his cheeks get sweetly pink, and he looks back at our little girl. "Not sure I'd call me *wise*, exactly."

"Because you let an eighteen-year-old seduce you?" I ask quietly once the nearby elderly lady reaches the end of the aisle. "Or because you fucked her bare and unintentionally spawned?"

The color in his cheeks rises. "Pretty sure I was fantasizing about the spawning part when I fucked you, so the intention to breed you was definitely there, but so was the intention to discuss it with you in the morning. The *unwise* part was falling asleep so soundly I missed your escape and didn't get a chance to take you to breakfast and convince you that *no strings* was a stupid idea."

My core ripples with delight at his words, and the box of cereal I'm holding slips from my fingers and falls into the shopping cart. He looks at me, his expression concerned and remorseful.

"Well," I say breathily as I try to get a grip on myself. "I was not expecting you to say that."

"And I was not expecting you to be eighteen, have a different name, or be this fucking ballsy. The truly unwise thing was probably taking you home with me, at all."

I stare at him and cross my arms over my chest. "Are you saying you regret it?" I ask, glancing at Viv.

Gunnar frowns. "Who could regret this?" He lifts her, so their faces are side by side. "No, I don't fucking regret it. I had a good time, and honestly, I already love this little nugget so much, I don't want to hand her back. I just... It's going to get complicated, and I regret not being more prepared for that. I feel like I stole your innocence and your youth."

"I'm an old soul, who lost her youth a while ago. And you do realize I chose to give myself to you that night. Right? That I *chose* to keep our baby? I made these decisions for myself. As an adult. You didn't steal shit. If anything, you *gave* me things."

Gunnar looks me over, and nods. "Okay. I'm pretty sure I'm still the villain here, but I appreciate the pardon."

I razz my lips at him. "At best, you have shades of being morally gray, which — lucky for you — is actually this season's hottest color. And so we're clear, I don't regret any of it, beyond being too chicken to tell you about Viv sooner. I'm grateful for how you were with me that night, and for how you're being with me now."

"Seriously?"

"Mmhmm." I try not to look at him too intensely, because he looks so fucking good with a tiny baby in his massively strong arms, I kind of want to see how many he can hold at once. Is it normal to want more babies so soon after having one? I mean, I fucking love Viv to bits, and I do want to have more kids — one day. But I didn't realize *one day* could come so quickly. It's not like giving birth is a super-fun experience, and it's still relatively fresh in my mind. I should be more wary, shouldn't I?

I glance at Gunnar and Viv again and feel the same tug in my loins, but it doesn't make a lot of sense to me. Before seeing him today, I may never have figured out how to tell him about Viv, and I definitely wasn't prepared for him to say he wanted to be involved. I don't know how to navigate a safe co-parenting situation. I don't really picture any father figure when I think about the kind of family I want to make. It's more like me taking care of my kids on my own — like Shelby. A simple, sheltered life, where there's no chance of some uncommitted guy getting close enough to then leave my kids feeling abandoned someday. Gunnar might stoke my feminine desires and make me feel confusing things, but I'm the only one I trust to stand by my babies through thick and thin.

We walk along in silence for a bit, occasionally adding groceries to the cart. I like watching what he chooses, but I can't decide what his choices tell me about him.

"You don't eat many vegetables?" I ask when he continually collects pantry-type items and no greens.

"I grow most things I need," he says with a shrug. "And I hunt. Mainly, I need ingredients. I like to bake, and meals taste better and are more nutritious when they're made from scratch."

Holy shit, did he just got hotter?

I look him over again, taking note of his rougher edges in a way I may have missed before.

"I always have plenty of fruit and veg, if you'd like me to deliver some to you?" he says. "I'd like knowing you're provided for and eating well," he adds, giving my sugary cereal the side-eye. "Could I do that for you?"

Is he asking me if he can take care of me? Is it too uncouth to say *hell, yes*? I'm a strong, independent woman, so why does the idea excite me so much? Do I like fresh vegetables that much, or is it him? I want to see him again. Feel pleasured and treasured and pampered; feel him inside me.

"That'd be nice," I say with a polite smile, doing my best to remain calm as my core begins to throb. "I'd appreciate it."

His face lights up, and he looks quite pleased with himself. "What kind of things do you like to eat?"

Is he asking because he'd go out of his way to indulge me?

"I eat anything," I say, still smiling.

He drops his gaze to my lips and makes a quiet humming noise. "That makes things easier."

"I like easy." I shrug. "The world can be plenty hard enough, without our trying to make it harder."

I push our shopping cart along, gathering the essentials I need, and I can almost pretend we're a little family.

An on-purpose, happy family, who share the responsibilities of daily living. Weirdly, I can imagine us with more kids, and every one of them would feel loved and wanted. It's not the kind of messed-up family situation that usually consumes my thoughts, where I do everything because my dad doesn't have a clue what day it is and barely acknowledges my existence.

For some reason, it's hard to imagine Gunnar being like that. Is it because he implies he wants to provide for his daughter and take care of me?

Even though he's completely obsessed with the baby girl he's just met, he keeps looking at me, too. And there's something about his gaze that makes me feel like I'm someone amazing, who should be awed or something.

He looks back at Viv and sighs so softly, I think his heart may actually be melting inside his chest. He's known her less than an hour, and he's head over heels for the girl.

I keep my smile contained and do my shopping, but it's hard to take my eyes off such a big, handsome man, when he's being so sweet and tender with a baby who looks impossibly tiny in his arms. "She's pretty cute, huh?"

"She's so fucking cute, I want to die," he says without pause. "You did some real good baking here, Jem." He beams at me briefly before holding Viv closer, in a protective cuddle, when another shopper walks past.

I want to say, *She gets the cuteness from you*, because he's being fucking adorable.

And it's sexy as hell.

I've never thought about guys acting all smitten with their babies, but it's fucking *hot*.

Or maybe it's him. With his sparkling eyes, rugged beard, broad shoulders, torn jeans, and a Pink Floyd Tee and under an open plaid flannel shirt. Rugged-rocker-mountain man-*god*.

I fucked that.

Well, mostly he fucked me. Hard. And bare.

An appreciative utterance leaves my throat, and he looks me over as I shiver.

Of course, I have to pretend I'm not craving his cock, so I don't look like a needy brat. "Frozen-food section." I rub my arms like I'm cold.

He glances at the ice cream nearby and grunts softly, but when he returns his gaze to me, it lingers on my breasts.

My nipples are hard as fuck, and the breast I didn't feed Viv with is now leaking through my — *his* — T-shirt.

"Oh, for fuck's sake," I mutter. I cross my arms over my chest, instantly overwhelmed.

Inside, I feel young and aroused when he treats me in a way that makes it easy to fool myself into believing I can handle anything, and that I'm cute and sexy and worthy of attention, but really, I'm this awkward, milky cow, who makes impulsive decisions, and as much as I want to do everything myself... I also want to be told I'm doing a good job and everything will be okay.

Since I got pregnant, my emotions can be all over the place, and the last thing I want to be doing is crying in the supermarket aisles, in front of a man I'd rather be impressing, considering he's probably going to demand a role in Viv's life, and there's no real excuse why he shouldn't be. I can already tell he's going to be a better dad than mine have been.

A wave of guilt hits me. I shouldn't have thought that — especially about a guy I barely know. My dads did the best they could, and I had an amazing childhood. For most of my life, my dads were wonderful.

Before they left and forced me to face everything alone.

The heartache I keep shoved deep wells to the surface in a rush, making it hard to breathe.

"Little Miss?" Gunnar says softly.

I meet his warm gaze and can't stop the tears from falling.

"It's okay, beautiful. Here." He juggles Viv like an expert, shrugs out of his shirt, and using one hand, drapes it around my shoulders and arranges the way it falls, to cover the wet circle expanding over my breast. "There. See? Nobody will know, but if anyone even looks at you the wrong way, you tell me, and I'll fucking sort them out. Okay?"

He gently brushes a tear from my cheek, and I suck in a shuddering breath and wipe my nose. "Thank you for being so nice to me."

Gunnar falters and takes a step back. "I..." He seems unsure of what to say next and closes his mouth as he frowns. "Jem," he says eventually, "you're the mother of my child, and I will strive to respect and care for you, because that what's best for you and for Viv. I'm not doing anything more than what any decent human should. You don't need to thank me."

Has it been so long since someone helped me that I forgot it's a thing that can happen?

I sort of want to cry even harder.

I'm definitely attracted to this man, but when he's being all supportive and kind and helpful, I can literally feel myself falling in love with him, and I don't want to. I don't want to rely on him, only to have him walk away.

That's all anyone does.

My gaze falls on Viv, sleeping in his arms. It's true love in his eyes when he looks at her, but I don't inspire the same kind of emotions in people. I believe he'll stick around for her, and that's the best I can hope for.

Maybe some casual physical stuff, if he's up for it, but no attachment. I don't have the energy to make and lose any more of those.

I sniff back my tears, clear my throat, and lift my chin. "Sorry. Hormones catch me off guard sometimes," I say dismissively. "Thanks for the shirt."

"You're welcome." He tilts his head and appraises me with concerned eyes. "You sure you're okay?"

I nod once. "I'm fine. I should really finish my shopping and get home, though. I have things to do."

10

GUNNAR

I'm not sure what happened at the grocery store, but Jem went from a warm, interactive, and charming young woman to someone with a quiet, colder, almost sullen demeanor, and I felt both awful and responsible for it.

I didn't want to leave her that way, but she gave me no choice. I offered to do every possible thing to help her, but it only seemed to make her more irritable, until she told me to back off. With volume. In front of everyone in the parking lot.

"I'm a strong, independent woman, and I don't need you to do anything for me, Gunnar Scott."

She would have left it there, too, had I not begged her contact details, so I could see my daughter again.

I still can't quite believe I have a baby.

My sister slapped me upside the head when I told her Viv was already two months old, but it's not like I didn't try for a different outcome. Jem was really fucking good at covering her tracks. She truly meant *no strings*.

Until she found out I knocked her up.

Initially, she seemed almost aroused and kind of into me doing it half-on-purpose, but now?

Now, I'm almost scared to get out of my truck.

I look at the house I've parked in front of, and then double-check the address Jem gave me. This is the place.

Cute neighborhood. Safe. Not too busy or too snooty.

She lives with another single mom — the actual Shelby, whose license Jem borrowed, to go out and meet... me. I'm glad she's not living alone, or with some other guy, but the way she described the arrangement irks me. Apparently, Jem and Shelby help each other out with stuff, which is great. Child care. Rent. Utilities. Great.

It's something else she said when she was explaining their living situation. Or rather, it's the way she said it. That's what grinds.

We don't need men.

It sounded like I was meant to take it personally.

And I did.

I have a baby girl. I want to be fucking needed. What's the alternative? Having Viv grow up to have a filthy old asshole rough-fuck a baby into her when she's barely turned eighteen?

Fuck that.

Where the hell is Jem's dad? Useless fucker. He should have been giving her love, so she didn't go looking for it in my neck of the woods. He could have kept her from my depraved clutches.

But then there'd be no Vivvy, and my heart fucking hates that idea. *Gah.* I close my eyes and collect my thoughts.

It is what it is.

What's the best way to handle this situation moving forward?

I need to be firm on what's right and wrong before I set foot in that house. I want to ease Jem's load and make her smile and give her what she needs, and not cross any boundaries she sets out, which is going to be difficult if she gives me fucking bedroom-eyes as often as she did last time we were near each other. I'm pretty sure she needs another hard fuck, and I definitely want to give it to her, even though I fucking hate myself for it.

She's so young. I'm appalled with myself, but eternally grateful she was at least fucking legal. What if she'd been even younger when she lied?

Bile burns my throat, and I shake my head. She wasn't. She's not. She's an adult. I'm allowed to want to fuck adults. Even the young ones with breeder hips and feeder tits.

I groan and rest my head on the steering wheel of my truck.

The sight of her, feeding the baby? The wet spot, spreading from the center of her breast to soak my favorite fucking T-shirt? The sweet scent of her milk when I leaned in close or smelled it on Viv? All those things affected me in ways I wasn't expecting.

If she hadn't burst into tears when she had, I would have turned on the charm, so I could get inside her again. The beast within me could hardly restrain himself at first. The urge to fuck her right then and there had been so strong, it was overwhelming.

Only her tears and having little Viv in my arms gave

me pause long enough to reason some sense back into myself.

I shouldn't want to fuck her like that. After what I already did to her life, I should leave her alone. And I will. It's for the best. *Don't fucking touch her, creep.*

As fierce and independent as she claims to be, she's young and fragile and off limits — especially if I want to keep things simple. She's allowing me into her life, but she made it clear she doesn't need me. I shouldn't even want the forbidden fruit.

But I fucking do.

I want to stick my dick right into her soft, warm center and fuck her full of cum again.

I growl at myself.

No fucking, and no *trying* to fuck her. Best behavior. That's it.

I'm only here to do whatever I can, to support my girls.

I open my door, get out of my truck, and retrieve the box of eggs, fruit, and vegetables from the back.

Jem answers on my first knock, and a rush of sweet cookie-smell wafts at me from inside.

"Hey," she says with a strained smile, wiping messy hands on the even messier cloth she's holding. "You were sitting out there a while. I could see you through the kitchen window." She tilts her head toward the room off the entryway.

"Oh." I lift the box I'm holding and ask with my eyebrows if I can put it in there.

She nods, and I hold it on my hip while I clear some

counter space for it. "I was just thinking," I say, as I stack dishes one-handed.

She rushes to help. "Sorry. I meant to tidy, I just…"

"You don't have to do that for me. I'm not fancy, and it looks like you're baking. Baking gets messy. Everyone knows that." I don't give a fuck about the state of the room, when the state of her is all I'm worried about.

She looks exhausted. There are dark circles under her eyes, her hair is one big tangle, her clothes are rumpled and stained, and I don't know why, but she looks hungry. Hungry and thirsty.

To avoid staring and making her feel self-conscious, I step around her and drop down to where Viv is wriggling and sputtering wet mouthy noises on a blanket under a colorful play-gym thing. *She* looks immaculate and well-cared for.

"Hello, beautiful girl," I coo and give her a raspberry kiss on her cheek that makes her scrunch her face and squirm. I tilt my head, as I look at her. "Did you grow, in a day?" I turn to Jem "Did she grow, or am I imagining it?"

"She grew," Jem says with a quiet groan. "It's like I put her to bed one size, and when I picked her up again, she was bigger. I don't know how it works, because it's not like she's sleep-eating. The physics doesn't make any sense. It's like she absorbs extra mass particles from the air around her while she sleeps, or something."

"You're switching to Growing Mode in your sleep, little sausage?" I say in a silly voice to Viv as I let her grab my finger. "What a good girl. Getting all big and strong. Look at these little muscles."

"What kinds of things were you thinking about in

your truck, for twelve minutes?" Jem scratches her cheek and leaves flour on her skin.

Her gaze is as shifty as her feet, and she seems nervous.

"Um... I guess I was giving myself a pep-talk about how to handle this whole situation, and I decided I would take it as it comes, and work with what you feel comfortable with," I say, almost absently, as I look her over more thoroughly. "Rough night?"

Her cheeks begin to color, and she runs her hand over her hair, leaving flour there, too. "Viv wanted to feed most of the night, so I barely slept. Is it obvious?"

"No," I assure her softly, though it's a fucking lie. "But I can watch Viv if you want to go shower or nap or... whatever you want."

Jem looks down at her Blind Melon T-shirt, holding it out to assess the stains. She moans and glances at Viv, and then at me. "I don't remember showering yesterday, so that's probably a good idea. You wouldn't mind?"

"Not at all. You go ahead. We'll be okay. Won't we Viviana Bea?" I frown. "When did you last feed her?" I ask Jem.

She feels her breasts absently, as her expression turns thoughtful. "About an hour ago? She'll probably want more soon. She's brought in a whole lot of milk after suckling all night, and she'll want to drink it," she says with a wince as she gingerly presses the top of one swollen breast.

"Hot showers are good for easing that, I hear. My sister used to release that way if she felt too full."

Jem stares at me. "I kind of like how much you know

about all this. I'm too tired to explain it, so it's a relief not to have to. You'll really be okay?"

"You'll still be in the house if I'm not. Right?"

Jem relaxes her shoulders and nods. "Of course. Um... thanks."

"Don't mention it." I wave her off. "Me and Viv want to spend some time getting to know each other, anyway. Isn't that right, little button?"

Jem looks between me and our daughter and smiles before heading upstairs.

I pick Viv up for a snuggle, and once I hear the shower turn on, I take a quick tour of the house.

I don't know where the other woman and her kid are or what kind of shit they do, but the house is a mess. There are toys everywhere, with no apparent system to contain them, and one of the armchairs in the living room has so much clean laundry on it, there must be nothing left in anyone's closets — which I can't dismiss as an exaggeration when I discover the piles of dirty laundry surrounding the washing machine.

My Nirvana T-shirt and flannel shirt are the only clean and folded things in sight, and I don't like it. They're sitting on the entryway table, as if ready to be taken away, and the fact that Jem would prioritize washing, drying, and folding them to return to me feels like she wants them the fuck out of her life — or wants *me* the fuck out her life.

"Well, I'm not going anywhere, Viv. You fucking need your Daddoo, so we'll have to show your mom I'm not some good-for-nothing deadbeat."

Viv doesn't agree or disagree. She's fallen asleep in the crook of my arm, like the fucking angel she is.

I go back to where I saw a baby sling hanging over a door and strap it on, to keep Viv close. Then I pull up my sleeves and get busy.

The dishes are done, and the kitchen smells of baked goods and something else that's more savory, both of which can be identified as incredibly wholesome and nutritious from their scents alone.

The toys have also been tidied into a corner, the laundry is folded, and there's a large, sexy man, mopping the dining-room floor, with a baby strapped to his chest.

I am *so* going to fall in love with this son of a bitch if he keeps coming around to do shit like this.

How long did I fall asleep for?

I walked out of the shower, feeling horny and light-headed. I lay on the bed to have a quiet moment to myself, but must have passed out for a while afterward.

It felt like late afternoon when I woke, so I threw on some clothes and rushed downstairs, freaking out that I haven't yet started making dinner for Dad and Shelby, and knowing I'll be waylaid even more, because my tits feel ready to burst with Viv's next feed.

"She slept that whole time, and you *cleaned*?" I ask,

waiting safely at the door to avoid the wet floor and Gunnar's sure and sturdy sweeps of the mop.

"She's been good as gold," he says with a smile, setting the mop aside just as Viv starts to squirm and make some waking noises. "You feel better after your sleep, mama bear?" he asks, pulling Viv from the wrap so carefully, I want to give him a medal. "I hope you don't mind that I poked my head in, to check on you," he says, glancing my way. "I started to get worried when I didn't see you after a while. I thought you might have fallen in the shower."

My face warms.

I woke still naked from the shower, with my towel barely covering me at all. He totally saw my ass. Probably my tits, too. Maybe... *Oh God*, my dildo was still on the bed. Did he *see* it? Oh, I want to fucking die.

"I..." *I* what? Do I pretend it didn't happen?

I raise my chin and clear my throat. "Thank you for tidying up. I didn't mean to fall asleep. Definitely not for as long as I did."

Gunnar lifts his gaze to me, as he jiggles Viv to settle her. "I'm glad you did. You looked like you needed it." He looks me up and down and nods. "Much improved. You hungry?"

My cheeks feel even hotter, and my nipples begin to prickle. "Oh, *fuck*. Here we go again."

I reach out for Viv, as my breasts start leaking through my clean tank top. Usually, I'd put breast pads in, to stop soaking my clothes with milk, but I was in a rush to get downstairs when I realized the sun was getting low in the sky.

Gunnar's gaze is like a fucking laser, and he stares at my chest — unapologetically, it would seem — which makes me burn up for a whole lot of other reasons that have nothing to do with embarrassment.

He hands me Viv, who's scrunching her face and turning pink. She's about to scream the house down. It's like she wakes up starving from every nap, and it's all I can do, to get milk into her as fast as possible.

I tug my tank top down, so my breast peeks out, and I shove it in her gob, just as she lets out a massive wail. My nipple takes her by surprise, and she whimpers once, and then sucks the hell of me, until I moan in relief as the over-full ache drains from my breast.

"I probably left her too long," I mutter, walking with her to the nearest armchair and pressing a cool palm to my other breast, to soothe the hot, swollen tissue.

Gunnar follows, watching everything, like he can't look away. He wets his lips, eyes on my free breast, as I encourage more milk from it, to ease the tight discomfort. That side is still covered, but the pale fabric has turned transparent from the spreading moisture, and the dark shape of my nipple is clearly visible, so I may as well be exposed.

I look from my breast to the sexy man I've captivated with it and feel suddenly powerful. And turned on by his interest.

Slowly, intentionally, I milk myself a little more, watching Gunnar closely, while he remains transfixed.

There's a giant fucking bulge in his jeans, and it's straining against the denim like it wants to escape. He likes my big milky tits. And I like him, enjoying the sight of me. So much.

The attention-seeking throb in my core makes me utter a soft sigh, as I massage my breast, milking myself far longer than I need to for comfort. "*Mmm. God*, that feels better. I was so fucking tight."

His gaze snaps to mine, and I pretend I'm innocent as fuck. "Oh. You don't mind, do you, Gunnar? I was so full, it hurt."

He absently slides his tongue between his lips, and the muscles around his throat strain as he swallows. "Ah... no." He sounds a little short of breath. "Of course not. You gotta do what you gotta do," he adds, glancing at my soaked, translucent tank top again, and then quickly looking away, like he's just now realized staring may be deemed inappropriate. So cute.

"Can I do anything else for you, while I'm here?" He runs a hand through his hair, as he looks around. "I made a lasagna with some of the stuff I brought over," he says before I can respond. "I hope that's okay. I didn't want you to feel rushed to do anything when you woke up, because I knew you'd be giving Viv all your time. And I appreciate that, Jem. You're doing a great job with her, and I know it's hard to do the other stuff at the same time. I can come over more often, if you'd like. Make life easier for you. I want to... make things easy."

His gaze drops to my breasts again, and to Viv, drinking. "She's a good feeder, huh? You must be giving her the good stuff. Nice and sweet." He cringes and clears his throat. "I — That sounded..."

My cheeks warm. "It's okay. I liked it."

He stares at me, his gray-blue eyes hungry. "Did you...?" He presses his lips together and seems to wrestle with his words, before he shakes his head and stands taller. "I should probably get going. I... Did I ask if you needed anything?" His voice is as strained as the denim covering his huge erection. "I meant to."

I want him to press that big dick against me. I want him to come closer, to say *goodbye* to his daughter, and I want to see longing in his eyes when he says goodbye to me, so his desire to fuck me is undeniable.

I rock on my ass a little, looking around for something to lure him in. "Um... would you mind grabbing me another shirt?"

He leaves the room and comes back with the Nirvana T-shirt I washed and folded, so I could return it to him. I wanted to fulfill at least some part of our no-strings agreement and cement the idea in his head that I don't need him to come into my life, thinking he can lure me into happy, blind dependence. I know how hearts get broken, and I'm not letting mine out to play that game. No, thank you.

Gunnar shakes out the shirt and offers it to me, and the way he stares me down means he got my message loud and fucking clear.

And he still went out of his way to take care of me.

Is this a fucking test? If I take his shirt, is it an admission that I like the way he behaved and want him to do it again? If I refuse it, it means I'd rather he keep his distance?

Does it have to be one or the other?

What if I want to play around with him, but not let him so close it'll hurt me when he tires of me and leaves?

What do I do with this offer if I want to feel in charge of the situation?

He stands quietly, patiently holding his shirt out, giving me time to make my choice.

The most I feel in charge is when I tell him what I want, and he does it.

I juggle Viv, so I can remove my soaked tank top completely, and then I hold up my free arm. "Will you help me into it?"

Gunnar's pupils are so dilated, his eyes are nearly all black. "Of course. Whatever you need." He steps closer and threads my arm through one sleeve.

He trails his fingers down my arm with the fabric, taking liberties with his task, to touch me more than is necessary.

He runs his fingers through my hair, and I shiver as he eases my head through the neck of the Tee. When I shift Viv onto my other breast, he *accidentally* strokes the one she left behind, while he guides my bare arm through the other sleeve.

"Thank you," I whisper, gazing up at him with mixed emotions. "That's all I needed." I like the way he touches me, as if I'm his, even though it's sort of naughty of him.

Would he be into a casual thing? Just sex? Would that be too confusing for Viv? She's young enough to not give a damn yet. Right?

Gunnar remains close, and all I can think about is his lips on mine.

"Can I kiss her *goodbye?*" he whispers, glancing at Viv briefly as she snuffles loudly at my breast.

Unable to speak, I nod and hold my breath, as he bows his head to kiss her curly head.

He closes his eyes as the tip of his nose presses to my breast, and he lingers, inhaling audibly and scuffing his beard over my sensitive skin. "I'll see you later, beautiful."

I can't help feeling like he's talking to me when he says it, but when he opens his eyes, his focus is on Viv, and he brushes his fingertips over her hair before he stands.

"Keep up the good work, little mama," he says, shifting his warm gaze to me with eyes I want to drown in. "You let me know if you need anything. Anything at all."

I nod, and he leans down to kiss my cheek.

On impulse, I turn into his kiss, grazing his lips with mine.

He stills. "Little Miss," he rumbles softly.

Weakened by a yearning for contact, I rub my cheek against his beard, asking for just a little more of his touch.

Then I freeze.

Dad's calling my name from next door, and he's getting louder and louder, as if he's been looking for me for a while.

12

GUNNAR

J em ducks away from me so fast, I back up in a hurry. I've overstepped the tentative welcome she laid out so beautifully for me.

She tugs her borrowed T-shirt down over her bared breasts and eases Viv from her suckling, to cover herself more fully. The baby goes over her shoulder, and Jem pats her back, while rising from the chair and looking around as if she needs something.

Her gaze stops on me. "I need to head next door for a few minutes. Would you mind holding Viv?" She's already handing over our little squawker, who is not a happy camper about losing her warm, milky nest so suddenly.

I rest Viv's little body against my shoulder and bounce a little, as I soothe and burp her. "Who lives next door?" I ask, annoyed that it comes out sharply enough for Jem to shoot me an irritable glare.

"Why do you need to know?" she asks.

I glare right back. "If some guy is yelling for the

mother of my child like she's a fucking dog who needs to get home, you can bet your ass I want to know about it," I say without hesitation. "Who is he?"

"My father," she says with a sigh. "I'll be back in a second."

"Your dad?" I start to follow.

She spins back to face me once we're out the door. "You asked if you could do something, and I'm asking you to stay here and hold Viv," she says, before calling over the fence that she'll be there in a minute.

She heads back inside, pushing past me on her way into the kitchen. Her eyes are slightly panicked, as she searches for something, and then her gaze lingers on the lasagna I made. She looks at me, and brings out a plate, cutlery, and a cake slicer she uses to divide and scoop out a section of the meal I lovingly prepared for her. "Thanks for making this. It really did make my life easier today," she says, before she heads out the door with the dinner plate.

"You have to feed him?" I ask, following her out.

"If I want him to eat," she mumbles, not turning back. "It's complicated. I'll be back in a few minutes," she says with a frown when I stay on her heels.

"Don't you think I should meet him?" I ask, pausing only briefly.

"Absolutely not." She whirls around and hits me with a forceful gaze. "He's not well, and your presence won't be appreciated."

"Well, he'll have to meet me sometime."

"Why? *Why* would he need to?"

I narrow my eyes. "Because I'm his grandkid's dad."

She squeezes her eyes shut in a wince. "He's too fragile to be a father, let alone a grandfather. Leave it be."

"His lungs sounded plenty sturdy to me," I mutter. "Probably where Viv gets it."

Jem shakes her head. "Just mind your own business, Gunnar. I haven't gone to your sister's house, to introduce myself."

"But she'd like you to," I say with a shrug. "She actually asked if I would bring you to dinner one Sunday, but I—"

"No," Jem says firmly. "I'm not looking for family ties. I've got plenty to deal with already, and you can't just barge in complicating everything." She glances at the house next door. "He doesn't know. Okay?"

I squint at her again. "Doesn't know what?"

"About Viv."

I look at our little girl, unable to comprehend. "I'm sorry. I... *What?*"

"He doesn't know I had a baby," she says quietly, her head down.

Still stunned, I shake my head. "How is that even possible? You live right next door. You were pregnant. And I didn't have the privilege of seeing you full-term, but you grew a whole baby inside you, so I imagine you looked *undeniably* fucking pregnant, Jem. And..." I hold Viv up as evidence. "How do you explain this?"

Jem takes a deep breath and runs a hand over her hair. "He's not really the observant type of late," she says quietly.

"What does that mean? Is he blind?"

She flinches and shakes her head. "I told you, he's sick."

"Like, terminally?" I ask, trying to keep my voice calm when disbelief and anger make it higher pitched.

She sighs and rubs her forehead. "No."

I don't know how to respond, because even if I was dying, I'd notice if my kid had a baby.

"What the fuck is wrong with him, then?" I ask. "Why doesn't he know? Why isn't he helping you? I honestly can't think of a single reason I wouldn't bend over backwards, to help my daughter if she was in your situation. I'd probably kill the son of a bitch who put you there, too."

Jem shrugs. "He used to be like that, but since Gabe left, Dad hasn't really been... present. His heart's too broken, and he needs help more than I do. He raised me well, and I can take care of myself."

"But he's an adult, and you're his child," I argue. "He should give a fuck. You think I would let this shit happen to Viv?"

Jem's gaze flicks to the baby, and then back to me. I can see in her face that she knows I'd never drop the ball if my kid needed me, but she lifts her chin and straightens her spine. "I may be his daughter, but I'm not a child, Gunnar. I'm grown. I'm a mom. I earn a living, and I take care of my family. I don't need you butting your nose in or making me feel shitty, for doing my best."

Her words hit me like blows. Making her feel inadequate wasn't my intention. Obviously, I struck a defensive chord. "I apologize if I made you think you're anything less than a strong, fiercely independent, and wonderful woman, Jem. I didn't mean to provoke an argument, and I'm sorry your father was so broken by your family's loss. This Gabe — he was your other dad?"

She nods. "He's the second of Dad's spouses to walk out on us. My mother was the first. I don't really know her or care to, and from her complete absence in my life, I'd say the feeling's mutual. Dad didn't blame her for leaving, since he only really figured out he was gay after she gave up her career and general awesome life to start a family with him, when apparently, she didn't even want kids." Jem stares at the ground and shrugs. "But Dad was head over heels for Gabe, and I was too. I thought we were a happy family, but in my senior year, Gabe just up and left us, out of the blue. It was a total shock — one Dad hasn't recovered from."

"What about you?" I ask gently, now realizing why she responds so well to attention and affection. She hasn't been getting any for months. And I know exactly how it feels, to be the strongest one left standing after a parent walks out on the family — the responsibility, the effort, the exhaustion and endless worry.

And her fucking mom left her too?

How fucking unlovable does Jem feel, after being walked out on *twice*? Is that why she pulls back when she finds herself leaning into the undeniable attraction between us?

I want to crush her to me in a big hug and tell her that time brings change and everything is going to work out fine, but she's still kind of fuming at me, I think. And who can blame her, when I've made her spill her secrets?

Her life is hard, so she simplifies where she can with

an M.O. of *no-fucking-strings*; she doesn't want me involved. I was the part of her life that was adventurous and fun, but the rest sounds really kind of shitty, and she wants to keep those things separate. Compartmentalized. I get it. I'm all too fucking familiar with the process.

It's survival, and it makes me want to hug her even more.

I snuggle Viv closer, instead. "I'm sorry, Jem. About all of it."

She nods and looks at the plate in her hand. "I'll be back in a minute," she says dismissively and leaves me to wait on the doorstep with Viv, who promptly begins screaming her head off.

I take her back inside, to calm her down, so Jem can do what she needs to do, without having to tend to a baby as well.

"It's okay, my sweet. Daddoo's got you. And Mama just filled your belly plenty, so there's no need to fuss. Except maybe about these soggy britches of yours." I say, patting her full diaper.

I change her butt — twice — and put her in a fresh onesie, because the last one didn't survive the explosion she made the moment I finished changing her the first time.

"All happy now, are ya?" I blow a raspberry on her belly, and she gurgles at me with a toothless grin. "Was your tummy making you a grumpy munchkin?" I ask.

She grabs at my lips, and I pretend to eat her hand.

"Daddoo's got the cutest baby in town. Doesn't he, beautiful? He kind of wants the prettiest little mama too,

Viv. Even though he knows he shouldn't and only seems to annoy her. You think it might happen one day?"

Viv blows spit bubbles at me.

"Helpful." I jiggle her gently, not wanting to wear the meal she just ate. "Pretty sure I'm being stupid. Mama's all hot and cold, and there's clearly a line she's not interested in crossing. She's way too young for the likes of me, and I don't need to make her life any more complicated than it already is. I don't want to make life harder for either of you."

I kiss her forehead and sigh. "The guy next door definitely needs to stand on his own two feet, so your mama can trust him to be there for her, though. He's going to need to learn about you and me for that to happen, little one. But don't you worry. You're perfect, and he'll have no choice but to adore you. If I'm going to make things work with Mama without causing added strain, it's me who'll need to win him over. And that's not going to be easy, because I could be as old as he is, and your mama's still fresh out of school."

I look around the place. "She's pretty grown up, though. Isn't she, bubba? She's a clever one; that's for sure. Savvy. Wise and sexy, like no girl her age should be. Wish that didn't float my boat so damn much. It'd make it easier to keep my distance."

Viv babbles right back at me, like we're having a conversation, and I snort softly. "You're going to be a little smarty-pants like her, aren't you, blossom? But Daddoo's not letting you anywhere near any big, old, nasty men like him. He's going to give you lots of love, so you don't have to go looking for it elsewhere. You think that might work for Mama, too?"

I think about what Jem really needs right now, and I want to kick myself, because it ain't me.

I take a deep breath and tuck Viv into my side. "Ready to go meet your pops, Viviana Bea? We're going to go rip the Band-Aid off and deal with the fallout, so Mama can start healing. It's going to fucking sting, but it'll be worth it, in the long run. She needs to feel some love from her people, or she'll teach you it's better to be alone. But it's not, Viv. People need people. I spent the last year figuring that out, and if I want to be one of Mama's people, I'll need to be initiated into the tribe. She's not going to like it, though. It'll be a trial by fire, so hold on to your li'l cotton socks."

13

JEM

I snap my head up, as Gunnar enters Dad's living room with Viv strapped to him in the baby sling.

"What are you doing here?" I ask through my teeth. "I told you to—"

Ignoring me, he walks straight up to my dad and thrusts his hand out — a non-verbal but very clear directive for it to be shaken. "Pleased to me you, Mr. Wade. I'm Gunnar Scott, Viviana's father."

I groan and jump to my feet, nearly spilling the last of Dad's lasagna into his lap, because he has zero appetite, and after coaxing him to take each mouthful, we were only halfway through.

Dad stares at Gunnar's hand, then at Viv, and finally at me. His eyes remain somewhat vacant, while I imagine the cogs in his once sharp mind slowly turn, to form a conclusion.

"Shelby's little girl?" he asks.

I glance at Gunnar, and my cheeks heat, as I nod. "Yeah, Dad."

WILD OAT MILK   125

"Congratulations," he says to Gunnar, slowly reaching to shake his outstretched hand.

But Gunnar pulls his hand away. He's staring at me, and he's not happy. "Shelby?"

"Nice girl," Dad says in a monotone, as he summons the mind to have a fucking conversation, despite my talking to his blank expression for the last ten minutes.

"Gunnar, can you please go back next door? My dad can't handle visitors currently."

Dad looks at me, and then at Gunnar. He sits up more in his chair. "I'm fine."

"Oh, really?" I take his plate to the kitchen and leave it there. "Then why am I practically spoon-feeding you like a baby? You've said two words to me since I came in, but now you want to talk, because a handsome man entered the room?" I growl and toss a damp facecloth in his lap. "You have sauce on your chin."

Gunnar says my name so softly, I want to cry, but I grit my teeth, force it down, and turn my anger on him. "I told you not to follow me."

"And I chose to disobey," he replies with a *what are you going to do about it?* look on his face. "This isn't okay, Jem. How long have you been doing this alone?"

"Since I had to. It'd be nice to share the joy, but being an only child is really fucking hard sometimes. Larger families probably do a lot of things way better, but I don't exactly have a big family lying around here. So I do what I can. Alone. At least I can do things my way."

"And this is the way you're choosing?" Gunnar asks, looking around. "It's too hard."

Viv gives a squawk of agreement.

"How is Shelby's little peach?" Dad coos, coming to life a little, like he sometimes has lately, when I have Viv with me.

His new antidepressants might actually be starting to help, but it's hard to tell, with so few good days struggling to shine through the bad. He seems to like Viv, but when he made the assumption she was Shelby's, I didn't have the strength to tell him the truth. Didn't want to send him reeling backward into despair, which is what Gunnar's about to do.

My heart's practically in my throat. "Gunnar, please."

"You're the baby's father?" Dad looks up at the large mountain man, without a clue what he's asking.

"I am," Gunnar says, not taking his eyes off me. "But she ain't Shelby's. I can see you're sad, and I know you're missing your man, Gabe, but you need to pull your head out of your ass and take a good, hard look at your daughter, sir. I know for a fact you haven't done that in over a year, and that's too fucking long to ignore your kid."

"Call me *David*." Dad looks between me and Gunnar. "Jemma, who is this man?"

I open my mouth to speak, but I can't form the words.

This is happening.

It's somehow both my worst nightmare and a fantasy I will replay later in my bed. Gunnar Scott is simultaneously fucking up my life *and* leading a white-knight charge for me, and I don't know whether to run or throw myself at his feet and worship him.

"I'm the man who got your eighteen-year-old daughter pregnant, and this is our baby," Gunnar says outright. "Jem hid her from me until this week, but I will be here for them both, for as long as they'll have me. I'm not sure if Jem's been intentionally hiding the truth from you, too. I don't understand how that could be possible. How she could hide an entire pregnancy from you, is beyond me. And the fact that you let her handle such a huge fucking event on her own is unacceptable. I need you to really hear me when I say she needs your help, because all you're doing is being a burden.

"I get that you've lost your spouse. Twice. But Jemma's lost those same people, and you made her grow up too fast. She has a baby, David. With *me*. Look at me. Do I seem like a suitable man for her?" Gunnar says, his volume escalating.

The voice in my head says, *Fuck yeah, hero. You're more than suitable. Swing your big dick back over the fence, and I'll meet you there.*

But my dad's voice asks, "Is this true, Buttercup?"

He hasn't called me *Buttercup* in nearly two years, and he says it so tenderly, my heart cracks open. He sounds the way he used to, when he'd turn my way and actually *see* me.

I look away, as the tears start to fall.

"Why didn't you tell me?" he whispers.

"You weren't here, for me to tell." I let some of my anger seep through in the words. "I doubt you'd have heard me. And I wanted to start a life beyond what I had in this house. A better life."

"With *him*?" Dad cries, finding some volume from somewhere.

"Alone, actually. But why not him?" I argue. "He's kind, and he's got the makings of a good father."

"To whom?" Dad asks. "You? He looks twice your age."

"He's *more* than twice my age," I snarl, ready to go head-to-head with him, now that he's acting like he's got enough pith to fight me back. "What are you going to do about it?"

"Forbid you from seeing him."

Cool, harsh laughter peels from my throat. "On what authority, Dad? I'm an adult. I don't even live here."

"You don't?"

"David," Gunnar says in a warning tone, "I don't want to yell at you in front of the baby, but I'm losing a lot of respect for you right now. You raised a smart and beautiful woman, but you fucking fell at the last hurdle, man. You need to pick up your game. You hear me? Sort your shit out, pay attention, and support your daughter the way she deserves."

"You speak as if you know what's best for her." Dad narrows his eyes to slits.

"Oh, I have an opinion about the need to prioritize your daughter over your self-absorbed misery, if that's what you mean. You're missing out on her life, and she's fucking amazing."

Fucking hell, I should not be getting wet between my thighs from this argument.

Dad looks between Gunnar and me, his gaze lingering on the baby. "You're right. I'll make an appointment with my doctor, first thing in the morning, and I'll make every effort to learn all that I've missed. I'm sorry, Jem."

I nod and keep my gaze on my toes. "So am I."

Dad shifts his focus to Gunnar. "But I think you'll agree that a man like you — who takes advantage of vulnerable young women, and irresponsibly impregnates a teen when he clearly has enough moral standing to know better — is not a man my daughter needs sniffing around."

"Define *sniffing around*," Gunnar commands, as he holds Viv closer. "Because I'm not abandoning my fucking kid, and I've given my word to Jemma that I'll provide any support she needs."

Dad's eyebrows twitch, and he almost looks impressed for a half-second. "I mean she's young, with her whole life ahead of her, and she doesn't need a man in his mid-life staking a claim on her. You've done enough damage already," he says. "Is she in love with you? Because, if she is, you had better make her stop."

"*Dad.*" I throw the nearest cushion at him. "None of this is your business."

"I agree," Gunnar says quietly. "But if it eases your mind, David, Jemma's already declared herself disinterested in shacking up with the likes of me. I believe falling in love with me is likely the last thing she wants, and I won't be encouraging her to change her mind. Had I known she was this young, I wouldn't have gotten involved."

Anger surges within me, and I stomp my foot. "Stop talking like I'm not here. Like I have no say in my own life." I march across the room and relieve Gunnar of our baby. "I don't love you, and I don't ever intend to. Loving people only leads to bullshit like that." I point at Dad. "I'm not going to do that to Viv. Ever. So don't even try, with your pretty face and helpful ways, making it look so tempting and easy. I won't fall into that trap. You can be Viv's dad, but you'll never be my man. I don't want one, and I won't ever want to depend on you. I fly solo on purpose, and if I need a dick, there are plenty of casual fish in the sea to keep me satisfied without you trying to yank on my line and leaving my heartstrings busted or tangled."

I turn back to my father. "You've ruined any fantasy notions of love I was ever going to have, so don't worry about me being stupid enough to be swept up in some useless, pathetic romance with Gunnar or anyone else. And you don't have any right to command my life, after what you've put me through. I will do whatever, and *whomever* I want."

"Except him." Dad nods at Gunnar. "Because he will respect what's at stake."

"Except me," Gunnar agrees. "Because you assumed I was prowling after Jem, but I'm actually already seeing someone."

My heart trips on his words, feeling bruised and heavy when it beats. "You are?" I ask.

He lowers his head and nods, clearly ashamed for his flirtatious behavior earlier. "It's sort of new, but she's sweet, and... more age appropriate," he says, practically kicking me while I'm down, which is stupid, because I meant everything I just said to him and Dad.

I don't love Gunnar Scott, and I don't ever want to.

Especially now.

"Well, there you have it, then," I say. "I'm sick of looking at you both, so I'm going home. Don't either of you expect to see me again for at least a week. I need a fucking break."

I kiss my father on the head. "I'm glad you're feeling better, but I'm going to hold you to your word that you'll get intensive with the doctors and consider *all* the options this time, because as mad as I am that Gunnar came over here"— I hit him with an extremely displeased look — "*against my expressed wishes*," I growl, "I'm glad he did. I don't know how much longer I could have gone on like this. Now we all know where everybody else stands, and that's perfect. Thank you, Gunnar, for making everything *abundantly* clear."

He looks from my father, to me, and then to Viv. His shoulders visibly rise with his breath, but he doesn't say another word. He presses his lips together, nods, and leaves.

And being walked out on feels as bad as it always does.

14

GUNNAR

I lied to the mother of my child.

I told her there was someone else. Like I've been able to get her out of my head since the night we made Viv together.

Dishonesty should never be the right path, and yet, lying was the right thing to do. Her father is right. She was vulnerable then, and she's still vulnerable. I need to protect her, not pervert her.

She played up a cavalier attitude about her finding other casual fish in the sea, but from the look on her face, she was pissed when I said there was someone else.

Probably because before her dad called out, I'd been about three seconds from sucking at her tits, to see what she tastes like.

A moan rumbles through me, and I barely get inside my cabin, before I'm stripping out of my clothes, to fall on my bed and fuck my hand.

I squeeze lube into my palm, and then push into my clenched fist, making it feel as tight around my cock as

Jem had been. This has been my daily fucking grind for a year. My guilty pleasure — fantasizing about blowing my load in her young cunt and waiting for her belly to swell with my growing seed.

The fantasy has gotten even more frequent since I found out I really did fucking breed her.

I release my cock and press my palms to my thighs, gripping them hard while I catch my breath. I shouldn't be entertaining these thoughts. She doesn't want romance and there'll be no happy ending to our story, but I can't help what I feel. I wish I could stop. I shouldn't want Jem's smart mouth and sweet, fertile young pussy.

She made me a perfect little angel, and I fucking cry when I think about what might have happened if I never found out about our baby girl. Already, Viv's a huge part of my heart; she and Jem both are. My girls.

I hold the image of them in my mind — Viv at Jem's breast.

The memory of her sweet scent makes my balls ache. I moan and shake my head, mentally moving the baby to her crib, to sleep, so I can imagine myself taking her place at Jem's pretty, milk-swollen tits.

My cock strains, and I clamp my fist back around it. I try to keep still, but my mouth is watering from imagining Jem's milk on my tongue, and my hips start to thrust of their own volition. I can't fucking stop.

I lie on my back and fuck myself harder, until the wet sounds are loud and all consuming. I close my eyes and think of Jem's gushing, juicy little cunt, spurred on by the sound of my slicked dick getting a good fucking rubdown.

She's so fucking pretty. And disinhibited. The way

she'd massaged her breast, to soak her tank top in front of me had lit an instant fuse in my cock. And she hadn't done it just a little. She drenched the pale fabric, so I could see right through to her dark nipple and *crave* it. And the look on her face while she did... It's like that's just what she wanted. She was turned on.

I thrust into my tight fist. "That's it, Little Miss. Get good and wet while you milk those fucking tits for me. Naughty girl. You fucking knew what you were doing to Daddy. You made him hard, and now you're going to take his fucking cock, like a good girl. Let me stretch that young little cunt, you sweet, breedy fuck.

"You had Daddy's baby, and you were acting like you want some more. Squeezing those beautiful fucking tits for me, until I could see everything through your wet clothes. Got fucking topless for me, too, like it's no big deal to flash your pretty tits my way, you fucking tease. I wanted to suck you so bad, and you fucking wanted it. I could tell.

"I should have fucking done it. Then. Or earlier, when I found you fast asleep with your tits out, a shine on your thighs, and a fucking glass cock next to you. You love a good fuck. Don't you, miss? Love that little pussy, full of cock and cum. Daddy should have climbed on top while you slept. Sucked those pretty tits, and fucked you bare, so you'd wake up pregnant again."

Tightness grips my balls, and I squeeze my cock harder, as the pressure builds to a blinding pleasure.

I roar as my seed shoots forth. It fills my fist to over-flowing, erupting through my fingers and all over my bare stomach. It catches in the trail of hair below my navel and smears over my skin, as I milk the last of it from my cock with a moan.

"Oh, sweet Little Miss. I like you way too much, for it to be good for you, and I fucking know it. Stay the fuck away from Daddy, darling. He's not fucking safe to be around, if he's thinking shit like that."

I groan and close my eyes.

"I'm sorry if I hurt your feelings by saying I had somebody else, but it's for the best. I have to at least try to keep my distance, baby girl."

JEM FUCKING HATES ME.

It's been more than a month since I ratted her out to her dad, and although she hasn't tried to keep me from seeing Viv, she's made it loud and clear that she thinks I'm a fucking douche-lord. She's not open to discussion about anything but our daughter, and even those conversations are like pulling teeth.

Mostly, I get the silent treatment.

A pouty face.

Angry, aggressive cleaning of shit that already looks pretty clean when I'm around.

Short, snippy responses when I push for answers to my questions about Viv.

She also returned the expensive phone I got her for her nineteenth birthday so she could make her little critter TikToks on something better quality than her old cracked one. Said she was happy with her current, much shittier phone, and that she'd upgrade when she's ready to, *not* when I thought she should.

I tried to reason with her, but she was making a point, and now she's basically been ignoring me for a month. And if she catches me looking at her too long, it's worse. It's like she goes out of her way to become even sexier, to show me what I'm missing, and then I'm scolded for wanting to look. I've taken to getting my fix from the few smiling photographs mounted on her walls.

My favorite picture is one of her holding a little hand-knitted baby sweater against her belly when she's heavily pregnant; so perfectly round and gorgeous with my child. She looks so happy and excited, and she's fucking glowing. The epitome of beauty.

Breaks my fucking heart that I never got to see her like that in person. I never got to slide my hands over her bump or feel Viv's first kicks. Could never be put to use, painting Jem's toenails for her or lending a steady hand to help her from a low chair. No rubbing her aching feet or her back. No holding her when she got scared or if her emotions got too much. No squeezing her hand and being there for the hard parts, so she knew she could trust me. She didn't want me there.

I was as useless to her then as she's making me feel now. Will I be reduced to only a cock in her mind? The sperm donor who helped start her family, instead of being a valued member of it? I don't want that. I want to be important to our family, and the more she acts like I can't be, the more I want it.

But I'm going to have to ride out the storm and hope for sunshine on the other side, which means showing up and doing what I can with what I have and navigating my family's needs as best I can. I'd appreciate more information sharing, but Jem's minimalist communication is making that hard. I have to rely on observations.

According to the big wall planner in her kitchen, she's had a few *Date Nights*, and I can guess what that means. She's young and pretty and enticingly open about her sexual appetite. I can't imagine she'd be shy about getting what she wants or needs on those dates. It's how it should be, but I can't help being disappointed.

She walks past, sees me looking at the planner, and doesn't even respond when I say her name. She just keeps on walking, so I give up on trying to talk with her directly. Instead, I talk to the room in general, so at least she knows *I'll* remain open to communication.

"I'm going hunting with some buddies this weekend, if you want to put in an order? I mean, I can't guarantee that we'll get what you want, but we usually get a few turkeys. Maybe a buck or a wild boar..."

No nibbles on that conversation, either. "I'll just share whatever I get with you," I say with a sigh as I settle myself back on the kitchen floor next to Viv, where she's batting at the brightly colored shapes dangling above her in and arch.

"I stopped by your dad's, to drop a few meals off, before I came over," I say, trying a different angle. "He's obviously not fond of me, but he seems a bit better. He told me what he's doing to help convince you he's invested in his health and your life. It must have been a tough decision for him, but you're his motivation, and he's definitely committed."

Jem says nothing and keeps organizing things in the pantry.

"Do you talk with anyone about him or any concerns you have? Because I'm good at listening, if that's what you need."

Silence.

"Not that you have to talk with me about it," I say, so I don't sound too pushy. "I know you're not into relying on others for support, but I hope you talk to someone."

No response.

I nod and lower my gaze back to Viv. "You probably have other friends you can talk to — people you prefer over me. Non-judgmental types you can talk about these things with, so you don't have to feel alone or worried about David. Neither of you seem to enjoy me too much, but I keep an eye on him too. Sounds like he's in good hands, and that he's beginning to feel more able to engage in his talking therapies now. That's good. Right?"

Nothing.

"I know electro-convulsive therapy sounds extreme, and that it gets a bad rap from the old days and movies and shit, but it's done in a totally humane way now and has proven very effective for treatment-resistant depression. Makes the brain release all those mood-boosting neurotransmitters in a flash so they can get to work. My neighbor back home in Montana swore by it, like it was a fucking miracle cure. It came up a lot when mom was having a rough time after my dad left. Mom was scared about it, and I was too young to know enough or weigh in with an opinion, but if I knew then what I know now, I probably would have tried talking her into it. She did respond to some of the meds eventually, though. Things got easier, and there wasn't any point talking about it after that."

Jem's silence feels too still, and I look up from Viv, to find her staring at me with the strangest look on her face. I have no idea what it means, so I ask. "Did I say something wrong again?"

She blinks at me a few times with her long, dark lashes, and then shakes her head. Her eyebrows dip into a frown, and she looks undecided about something — probably about talking to me, because when her expression smooths out again, she asks, "Your mom had depression?"

"Yeah," I say quietly, not wanting to do anything to jeopardize the first attempt she's making to actually engage with me.

She looks at me with interest, but it's not the kind I was craving.

"How old were you?" she asks.

"It doesn't matter." I turn back to Viv, so I don't have to keep pining for glimpses of her mom's smiles. My little blossom is pretty liberal when it comes to sharing her dribbly grins, and I'll lie on the floor with her and ham it up all day long to bask in that cuteness. "The point is she got better, and your dad will too."

"Why won't you say?"

I stay quiet for a while, and then sigh. "I was young. But I don't want you thinking ill of my mom because of the position I was put in. It wasn't her fault. I handled it, and we moved on. I only meant to say that I'm glad your dad's on the mend."

"Thank you," she says quietly. "It is good. He's still mad at me, though."

"He's mostly mad at himself," I assure her. "He let you down, and it'll take time for him to forgive himself. Whatever moody shit that currently looks like, it'll pass. Especially when he realizes how well you're doing for yourself. He's also hung up on your not going to college, like y'all planned, but it's not like you can't ever go if you decide to. I'll help you with Viv. He would too, probably. He loves you, and he's doing his best to fix things."

She mumbles her agreement, and then sighs. "I've been taking Viv over with me more often, and he may actually ask to hold her at some stage. I don't know. It's all kind of tense."

I nod. "I'm sorry I outed you without warning, but I'm not sorry everything's out in the open. It needed to happen."

She glares at me. "That's true enough, but I'm going to stop talking to you again, because I'm still fucking mad at you for not respecting my wishes."

"I know. But it was for the best."

"You don't get to decide what's best for me, Gunnar."

I smile at her. "You're right. But speaking as the guy who didn't get a call about your having his baby, I can assure you, time and knowledge matter. I would have responded a lot less favorably if you'd left things until Viv was old enough to introduce herself to me. I'm sure you've spent some sleepless nights, worrying about your dad finding out, but now you can rest easier."

"So I should be thanking you?" she asks with an arched brow. "I should be happy you bulldozed your way into my life, without a thought to handle things more delicately?"

"You be whatever you want to be, Jemma Wade. But don't assume I don't think about what I do before I do it."

She huffs. "Oh, so the other day, you thought it'd be a good idea to get all close and hot, copping a feel and leading me on when you already have a girlfriend?"

"*That's* why you're so grumpy with me? You're jealous I'm seeing someone else? Did you want me to touch you more?" I'm pushing her, so she'll shut me down with a *no*, but *my God*, I want her to say *yes*.

"I don't need you to touch me. I do fine all by myself." Pink blooms in her cheeks. "And I have my pick of the guys lining up to touch me when I go out. I just think it was inappropriate for you to touch and kiss me when you're not single, and I don't appreciate becoming the bit-on-the-side in some asshole's sleazy game."

I nod along, validating what she's pissed about — to a point.

"Technically, I only kissed you on the cheek," I remind her. "It was you who turned it into something more. And you're not some side-piece, you're the mother of my child. No matter who I see or what I do, you're at the top of my priorities."

Viv starts to fuss, so I pick her up and get to my feet, to bounce with her.

"But you're right," I add. "I shouldn't touch you in ways that blur the lines of our relationship, and I gave your father my word that I would keep my dick in my pants."

"Ooh. Big hero. What an honorable man," Jem says,

rolling her eyes. "As if I'd want that filthy fucking thing, anyway. I'm lucky I escaped it the first time with a healthy baby, instead of syphilis or some shit. I hate you and him both, for assuming I need more useless men in my life. You can take your stupid T-shirt and get the fuck out of my house. Now."

She marches to the front entryway, grabs my clean and folded Nirvana T-shirt from the side table, opens the door, and throws it outside.

It hits her dad in the face, but he barely seems to notice.

His face is damp, his eyes bloodshot and unfocused.

"Dad?" Jem's voice softens instantly, and she steps out to greet him. "What's happened? Come inside."

She guides him in and settles him into an armchair, while trying to coax words from him. She feels his forehead, checks his pulse, loosens his cuffs and his collar, and holds his hand, like he's the child. It's no wonder she appreciates anyone fucking thinking about her and her needs. I am a complete tool for taking advantage of that.

It takes a few minutes for David to find his words, but the moment he says, "Gabe had a massive heart attack," Jem sinks to her knees beside him, like she took a huge hit.

"They... I... I'm his emergency contact. He's in the hospital. In New York. *New York*," he repeats the words in a whisper. "He's stable, but he's... I have to go to him."

Jem looks up with a frown. "No. He made his choice. He's not allowed to need us. Pass the buck to Auntie Glam. She'll make sure he's okay. You're barely out in daylight. Don't throw yourself under a bus for that man and get hurt all over again, just because he didn't change a name on a stupid form."

Jem's father stares at her. "That man helped raise you. He's your father, and you'll—"

"He *left* me," she says through a tight jaw. "He walked away from both of us and ruined our family, and he can die, for all I care." She claps a hand over her mouth, clearly shocked by her own words. "I didn't mean it," she says, bursting into tears.

Viv joins in, screaming at the top of her lungs.

Jemma looks from our baby, to me, and then to her father, and she runs. Straight upstairs.

A door slams, and I meet David's gaze, as I do my best to calm Viv. "How do I make this easier?"

15

JEM

I dug in my heels, but Gunnar helped Dad wear me down. They've convinced me to travel.

Gabe's in Intensive Care, Dad's a fucking mess, and I'm at war with myself over whether I should let myself care, but Gunnar has calmly advocated the best course of action for each of us from a place of love and support. I know it's for the best if I go to New York to support my dads and address the rifts between us, but I'm uncomfortable admitting to Gunnar that he's right.

Half of me wants to fight him on it. The other half is weirdly impressed by his pulling my family together in a crisis. It's how families are meant to work, but I doubt it'd be happening without him nurturing it.

My hands are shaking, as I check Viv's overloaded diaper bag again. I hand it over to Gunnar, not ready to let go. Dad and I are going without Viv, and I'm sick about all of it.

I'm scared for Gabe at the same time as being livid about even giving a shit. I'm annoyed at Dad and Gunnar for making such a good fucking argument for leaving Viv behind, because Dad definitely can't make the trip without support, a hospital is no place for a baby, and I can't exactly shock the hell out of a man with a major heart condition by showing up and saying *Hey, Gabe. The little girl you abandoned got lonely, spread her legs for a real daddy-type, and popped out this little firecracker.* Dad's terrified Gabe'll have another heart attack if we spring it on him, and after what I said...

"I couldn't express enough breastmilk to last the whole weekend," I say on the verge of tears, as I hand Gunnar the can of milk powder. "I don't even know if she'll take a bottle. Shelby hasn't had any luck so far, when I've been out."

"We'll be fine, Jem," he assures me. "I'll make sure she's fed. You don't need to worry about her. Just do what you need to do, and come home safely, okay? Did you pack your pump, to keep yourself comfortable over the weekend?"

I pause to think, and then run back upstairs, to make sure, because I don't actually remember putting it in my overnight bag.

I breathe a sigh of relief when I find the breast pump near my toothbrush, which is still on the counter in my bathroom. I put it there to remind myself to get it, but that was clearly a flawed plan.

I pack them both, bring my bag downstairs, and set it next to Dad's. "Nearly forgot my toothbrush," I mumble, not wanting to admit how helpful Gunnar actually is.

He acts as if he could handle any situation, and it's a relief to know I can trust him to care for Viv and do anything she needs. He's good at that — a great dad. And even though I'm still annoyed at him for the way he handled things with telling my dad and for making me feel like a fool for wanting him, I know he'll do whatever needs to be done. It's how he is.

He's been pretty supportive about the whole Gabe issue — and with Dad's situation. I can't stop thinking about how he went through a similar thing with his mom. Only he had a little sister to care for when his dad left. And he was younger. Still a kid. How hard must that have been for him?

I was forced to grow up fast, but I was almost seventeen when Gabe left. Nearly an adult. Gunnar would have lost his childhood overnight. No wonder he's rough around the edges but responsible as fuck. He's a provider. Steady and dependable — even if I don't want to depend on him, I can if I need to.

Damn that sexy fuck, for being so reliable and consistent.

I'm beginning to think that kind of thing may be my man-kryptonite, which only makes me grumpier about the whole his-being-with-another-woman thing.

"Good luck," he says, handing me Viv for one last cuddle when the Uber driver pulls up out front, to take us to the airport. "I hope it all goes well and that your other dad gets better real soon."

"*Gabe*," I correct him. "He lost the right to be called *Dad* when he walked away from his daughter."

Gunnar dips his chin and presses his lips together, as he loads my bags and Dad's into the back of the Uber. "Maybe he thought he was doing the right thing," he says quietly when he takes Viv back from me. "Maybe you can ask him about it. Because no sane man would cut ties with you, unless there was a damn good reason, Jemma Wade," he says.

Is he talking about himself?

I stare at him a moment. How can he claim that? Like I'm so damn special. It makes it sound like he wants me, and it's not right. In fact, it's deeply unsettling.

He smiles sadly and waves Viv's pudgy little hand at me. "Take care, Mama Bear," he says, as I'm climbing into the car. "We'll see you when you get back, and hopefully, we'll have bagged enough game to fill your freezer."

I stop, with one foot in the car and one on the curb. I forgot all about his hunting trip. "You can't take Viv *hunting*."

Gunnar chuckles. "She is a bit small still, it's true. I won't take her into the bush with a gun. Don't worry. I'll just hang out with the guys, and then let them fill the freezer for us. It'll be fine."

I tighten my grip on the car door, and the urge to abandon my plans for New York is so strong, I set both feet back on the sidewalk. "Is it a *drinking* weekend?"

Gunnar watches me closely. "There may be a sensible amount of beer for post-hunt-refreshment purposes, but if it eases your mind, I won't partake, and there will be no drunk-driving, I can assure you. Jason lost his sister that way, and it scared the shit out of all of us."

I study him for a full minute, before Dad clears his throat. "Either you trust him, or you don't, Jem. Which is it? Has he tried to touch you since I told him not to?"

"What the fuck does that have to do with anything?" I growl at my father.

"If he's a man of his word, then you're getting in the car and we're going to see your sick father. The man who taught you how to swim, ride a bike, and drive. The man you do in fact love, despite trying your damnedest not to. Without Gabe, you would've been stuck with only me, and we all know how that's turned out, so unless you have a damned good reason not to trust this man, we're going. Has Gunnar made a move or not?"

I meet Gunnar's gaze and sigh. "I know where you live. You take care of our girl, or I'll use some of the more brutal skills Gabe taught me about hurting the tenderest parts of the male anatomy."

Gunnar's eyes sparkle, and he wets his lips as he nods. "I'm a little curious about those skills, but I'm not so curious I'll push the boundaries. You don't have to worry about Viv. I'll take good care of our girl, and you know it. Go babysit your dads and teach them a thing or two about how to parent."

"*Hey,*" Dad scolds from the car, making me smile.

Gunnar grins and makes Viv wave at me again.

Stupid, sexy man and his reassuring ways that make it hard to hate him.

16

GUNNAR

M ilking kink.
It's a thing. Like, *officially*.

I did not think a hunting trip to Ben's farm would give me answers to the questions I've been asking myself, but spending time with Ben and his young, lactating fiancée, Maggie, has been eye-opening, for many reasons.

I'm not a freak for getting a hard-on over my teen-mama's milky tits. There's a whole bunch of other people into this kind of thing, and I have to say, I'm fucking relieved.

Well, sort of.

Viv flat out refused to take formula from a bottle, and screamed until her little body was shuddering in an exhausted sleep, so when she woke up starving, I let Maggie breastfeed her.

The guys *all* got fucking hard watching Maggie bare her milky tits.

Apparently, Ben and Maggie worked together to bring in her milk, and Ben said it was like throwing gas on

the fire when it came to their sex life. From what I saw —
which was a *lot,* because Maggie's so open with her sexu-
ality — he was telling the truth.

My mind has been fucking blown, and I'm not alone
in that department. The guys are fucking buzzing from
our weekend, and only Viv is quiet, sleeping soundly
with a full belly and the smooth motion of Vince's big
truck.

I straighten one of her little socks, and smile as Jason
groans again. "Did that all seriously just happen?" he asks
for the fourth time. "I thought we'd walk away from a
hunting weekend at Ben's with some game in the back,
but we got a lot of fucking bonus shit, boys. Got ourselves
a live porn show and a sperm-donor checklist. Where the
hell did Ben find that woman?"

"*She* found him." Daryl snorts. "Remember that
woman he had, a while back? Solo mom? Had a daughter
who was about nine or ten? Well, Maggie's that girl, all
grown up, with a fucking mind of her own and a love for
Ben's firm but fair hand."

"Oh *fuck.* That's who she is?" Jason mutters. "All
grown up and milky as fuck. What the hell is *that* kink,
and why the fuck am I hard, just thinking about it?"

"Not the only one," I mumble. I sigh and look out the
window.

"If you liked it, then what's up your ass about it?"
Daryl asks. "Still pining for that long-lost woman from
your one-night stand? She was all you could talk about,
until you had Viv to gush over. She the kid's mom? What
was her name again?"

"Shelby," Jason and Vince say in unison.

"That was a fake name," I say quietly.

"No denial that she's your baby mama, then? Are we ever going to meet her or learn her real fucking name?" Daryl asks, folding his arms over his chest. "Out of nowhere, you drop the news you had a surprise baby with some mystery woman, and then you demand we respect your privacy. But we're your oldest, closest friends, and we don't keep secrets. How fucking private do you need to be?"

I close my eyes. It's time I admit to my shameful fucking behavior. "I've only told y'all the bare minimum about Viv's mom, because I don't want any of you assholes to even speak her name, let alone say a fucking thing about her." I chew at my thumb nail and stare out at the countryside as the cab fills with silence.

Daryl whistles. "She's right up under your skin, huh?"

I glance at Viv and then press my head to the cool window. "I've got it *bad*, guys," I admit, banging my head against the glass a little. "This girl is amazing. For various reasons, I can't be with her, but I want to be. So bad. And she's the one who sparked a massive milky craving in me that I didn't have words for, before this weekend. It's not just a *lust* thing, either. I think I fucking love her."

Everyone falls silent.

Jason swivels around from his position riding shotgun. "You don't fall in love."

"I know," I admit quietly.

He shakes his head. "Vince falls in love every fucking day, but you *never* fall, Gun."

"*Hey*," Vince says, but Jason gives him a challenging stare, and he shrugs. "Often. Not every day."

Jason concedes with a nod and turns back to me. "Spill your guts, bro. Who is she? Nobody's going to run their mouth about her if you're in love with the girl."

"Her name is *Jem*." I heave another sigh. "It was meant to be a one-night stand with no strings attached, and I met her in a bar. She was young, so I tried to send her on her way, but she..." I shake my head and utter a soft groan. "She's really something, and I couldn't resist. I fucked her all night. Broke a condom and loved the fucking sight of her creamed pussy so much I fucked her again in her sleep without protection before I woke to find her gone."

"You fucked her bare in her *sleep*?" Daryl growls. He seems upset as he looks me up and down. "Dude, that's fucking dirty. I know you fucking listened to the lecture my mom gave us about consent."

"I was given consent when she was awake," I assure him. "She told me I could do whatever I wanted with her, no matter what state she was in, as long as I made it feel good, and I believe I did. She made all the right sounds, rocked closer, and rippled around my cock when I came inside her."

"She does sound fucking special." Jason gives a grunt of approval.

"The fucking-her-bare part was kind of nonconsensual," I admit quietly. "But the previous condom had broken, guys. She was already full of my boys." Stuck in the leg of my jeans, my cock swells and creeps further down my thigh. "I fucking loved it, too. Until I woke up without her. I tried to find her afterward, but she'd vanished. What I didn't love, was finding her again — *by accident* — nearly a year later, with my fucking baby in her arms."

The boys hiss and *ooh*, like they understand the pain of that.

"She faked her name and her experience, and she's still younger than what her ID said at the time." I squeeze my eyes shut and confess all my sins. "She only just turned nineteen."

The boys make a range of noises about that. They know Viv's three months old, so the *oh-shit* long whistle and the nervous *ho-ho-ho* laugh, after doing the math out loud, don't make me feel any better about what I did.

"I know," I say. "She was legal, but only barely. Safe by a few fucking days, but it's just as bad. Actually, it's worse, because now I know the truth, and I still fucking want her. She's so pretty and smart and funny and filthy and just... solid — you know? She knows what she wants, and she goes out and gets it. She's a great little mama, and I... *God*, I want to suck her milky tits, and then fuck her hard over a log or something."

"Ben's Maggie is only nineteen, so it's not like you're the only guy getting freaky with someone half your age. And that girl knows her fucking mind too. Maybe the young ones are smarter and more confident than we were at that age." Jason chuckles and cranes his head, to look at Viv. "You want to make more of these little screamers with this *Jem*?" he asks me.

"Yeah. I can't, though. She's too young to be saddled with all the kids I'd want to grow on her. She doesn't want me. Even if she did, I promised her dad I wouldn't fucking touch her. That made her pretty angry. She basically said that we're stupid men, and it's only her business who she fucks, which is true enough. But I'm an idiot with an ego, so when she said she could get plenty of casual dick elsewhere, I told her I was seeing someone else. That pissed her off even more, but it turns out, I may need the extra layer of protection her hatred gives me, to keep me from being weak and pursuing her, because I really, *really* want to fuck her, man. And not once. Like, forever, and shit."

I push my fingers into my hair and lower my head to my hands. "And now I have to tell her that I let Viv suck on someone else's tits. I'm going to have to ask her about providing sperm for Ben and Maggie's baby, too. I feel like I need permission."

"Hey, what happens on the farm, stays on the farm," Jason reminds me. "You're not with her. You don't have to feel guilty about doing shit with your cock. It ain't hers, and she said she doesn't want it."

Hearing that truth is like another punch in the guts. I hang my head. "I know. But I don't think if I can donate sperm if she's against it. It kind of feels like my balls belong to her."

"It certainly seems that way from here." Jason snorts a laugh. "Why don't you convince her young ass to give you a shot, tell her dad you changed your mind, and then fuck her. Or don't tell him."

"It's more complicated than that. Both her dads are sick, and I can't rock the boat and create drama there. Their family is on the fucking rocks as it is. And I'm a father now, guys. I can't go doing shitty things, like fucking Jem behind their backs. Not that she'd let me fuck her, anyway. And I feel like she's going to get possessive and weird over the Maggie-feeding-Viv thing, so that'll be another strike against me."

I look out the window, at the world whizzing by, and feel even less in control. "I don't know if I'll ever be in a position to get another shot with her, truth be told. I mean, she didn't even tell me she had my baby. I ran into her at the store, saw the baby, did the fucking math, and demanded answers. What if she was never going to tell me? She's made it clear from the start that she doesn't need me, and she doesn't *want* to need me, and everything is just fucked."

"Maybe give it some time," Vince says. "Things are obviously a bit complicated right now, but maybe they'll be different in the future. Let the dust settle, and then see where things lie. And in the meantime, curb your milky little desires elsewhere. She already thinks you're fucking other women, so why not do it?"

"Because it doesn't feel right."

"Ah, unrequited love," Jason says with a smile. He settles back into his seat, facing forward again. "Nothing a few whips, collars, and ropes can't resolve. Maybe she'd be into it if you strapped her to the bed, sucked her tits, and left."

Vince alternates between giving him several stern glances and keeping his eyes on the road. "I worry about you."

"You should," Jason says with a grin. "Drop Gunnar home first. I want a look at this Jem girl."

"Fuck off. She's not home yet, and you're not invited for a sneak peek. I'm not Ben, and I won't be parading my girl's tits and ass around, or spreading her cunt so you can see her getting juicy. She's the mother of my child. I don't care if I can't fuck her; she's still mine."

"Sounds like she's the kind of independent woman who might have something to say about that, Gun." Daryl smirks, before he turns to look out his window. "And you may be fake-dating a fictitious woman to throw her off, but what are you going to do if she gets a boyfriend her own age?"

Cold sweat breaks out on my brow. "I don't even want to fucking think about it."

Gunnar is waiting on my doorstep when we return, and I jump from the car and run toward him. "Why are you out here? Is everything okay?" I drop to my knees next to the baby bouncer to get my first glimpse of Viv in three days.

"Hey there, Viviana Wade, cutest tot in town. Look at you," I say, pulling her into my arms for a cuddle. "*Holy moly*, girl. Did you grow again? Are you trying to catch up to your daddy?"

"*Daddoo*. I prefer *Daddoo*," Gunnar corrects me with a frown and a distant look in his eyes. "For Viv," he adds, and I gulp when I think about how we used the word *Daddy* before. "I um..." He pauses, watching Dad get our bags from the trunk. "You need a hand, David?"

"I got it," Dad calls back. He sets my bag down near us, nods at Gunnar, and then heads for his place.

"So how did it go?" Gunnar asks, his tone soft.

"I don't really know how to answer that." I snuggle

Viv, and then lift my shirt, to latch her on when she starts mouthing me through the fabric. "Okay? Sort of."

The muscles in Gunnar's neck strain as he swallows, and he looks away. He gets off the stoop and dusts off his jeans. "*Okay* is better than bad, I guess," he mumbles.

"It may become bad," I say quietly, so Dad won't hear. "Gabe's coming home to convalesce, in about a week, and Dad's going to be heartbroken all over again if they can't get over themselves."

I tilt my head, to look up at Gunnar, and squint from the late-afternoon sun. He watches my dad going inside his place, and keeps watching even after the door closes. He doesn't seem to want to look at me, for some reason, and I'm kind of too tired to wonder about it. "I asked Gabe why he left, like you suggested," I say.

Gunnar raises his eyebrows and turns his attention back to me. "You did?"

I nod and pat Viv's baby booty, to check the state of her diaper. It's dry. And she seems happy. She's been well looked after. "He'd been gambling," I say. "Ran up some debt with the wrong people — under his own name, but he was scared it might come back to us. So he left, sought help for his addiction, and he's been working himself to the bone, to pay everything off. Hence the heart attack. He was too ashamed to tell us, but fate forced his hand. So... it's not a great excuse for him to leave, but it beats the hell out of his dumping us because he doesn't love us."

Gunnar bobs his head while he's listening. "Men do weird shit for love, sometimes. And he's coming home in a week?" he says, still looking over at Dad's place. "I can meet him then?"

"I suppose. Are you okay? You seem tense. Did you have a rough time with Viv?" I ask, searching his face for signs of baby-related trauma from sleepless nights.

He shakes his head. "She's a good girl. She barely screamed at me after the first day trying to use a bottle."

I breathe a little laugh. "She does have a wicked set of lungs." I glance up and see Shelby through the kitchen window. I wave at her and Jaxon. "How come you're waiting outside on the stoop, when Shelby's home?"

Gunnar shrugs. "I feel weird about women called Shelby these days, I guess. She seems nice, and the kid's cool, but I... it's nice to hang out when it's just Viv and me."

He drops his gaze from my face to where our girl is feeding, and I could swear he's blushing when he looks away again. "I wanted to ask you about something, and you probably don't care, but it doesn't feel right, not asking."

I give him a sideways glance. "Sounds serious. Should I be sitting down for this?"

He looks me over and runs his hand over his beard. "Sorry. My head's..." He makes a twisty hand gesture near his ear, and then reaches for my bag. "I should let you in the door, to get settled." He apologizes again and opens the door for me.

Still feeding Viv, I walk inside and head upstairs, to my room. "I could do it myself, but would you mind bringing that bag up here for me?"

Gunnar does as I asked, following me up. I settle onto

my bed and switch Viv to the other breast, because my tits have not felt normal since I left her. I tried to empty them as often as I could, but expressing with a pump isn't the same, and I may have brought in more milk than she actually needs by using it as much as I did. Though she is bigger, so maybe it'll be a good thing.

"What is it you wanted to ask me?" I say, when he retreats a little.

Gunnar wets his lips, like he's nervous. "Okay. So, the friends I went to see — Ben and Maggie... I grew up with Ben. Maggie's his fiancée, and they live on a farm, out in the back sticks. Like, deep in the mountain range behind... It doesn't matter. What does, is that they're trying to have a baby, but Ben's kind of sterile. There was a whole *mumps* thing — his folks didn't believe in vaccines, it wasn't pretty, and the poor guy can't have kids. But they really want them, and—"

"If you're asking if you can give them Viv, the answer is *no*," I say with a chuckle.

Gunnar's eyebrows plunge. "Of course they can't have Viv. But the thing is, they asked us — me and the other guys — if we'd donate some sperm, to help out, and I felt weird about it, because I don't like knowing I may have a kid out there I couldn't help raise. Because what if my baby needed me? Right?"

He's so passionate when he talks about his parental responsibilities. Does he know how fucking hot that is? Does he say this shit to his girlfriend? Lucky bitch. I hope she appreciates it.

"But then everyone said we could all donate and inseminate on the same day, so nobody would know whose sperm actually makes the kid, and at the end of the day, it's Ben's and Maggie's and nothing the fuck to do with me — which I said I was okay with, because I know Ben will be a fucking great Dad, and Maggie's sweet and loving, and they'll be good parents, but I kind of wanted to ask if you had any strong feelings about it?"

I stare at him. "*Me?*"

He nods.

"You want to know if I have feelings about you donating sperm to help your friends?" I ask, slowly and carefully, in case I missed something.

Gunnar nods again. Is he sweating? He's wiped his brow twice since he got to my room, and it's not that warm in here.

I tilt my head to view him side-on. "Why are you asking me? Shouldn't you be more concerned about what your girlfriend thinks?"

That makes him stand a little straighter. "Um... It's not that kind of relationship. We're not really... It's not like she'd want..."

I hold up a hand to stop him. "Are you implying *I* want your sperm?"

He tenses his jaw and shakes his head. "I don't know what I'm implying."

I raise an eyebrow at him. "It's *your* sperm, Gunnar. Do whatever you want with it. Why would I care what you do with it?"

He shrugs. "I don't know. You're the mother of my child. I value your opinion. I... I'm processing, I think. Ben's always wanted to be a dad, and it'd be pretty sad if he could never have a little Viv of his own. It makes me feel a bit squishy." He says the last part in a whisper, rubbing at his chest. "I'm going to help them do it."

Totally confused, but not immune to how adorable he is when he gets *squishy* inside, I stare at him. "Okay?"

Gunnar nods and takes a step backward. "I should go."

He doesn't. Instead he lingers by the door.

"Was there something else?" I ask.

He takes a deep breath and scratches the back of his head. "Yeah. I... um... I fixed the shower. Shelby said it was leaky, and the pressure was shit. I had the time, and Viv was happy, so I fixed that. I figured you'd probably want a good shower when you got home. I always feel like that after traveling, anyway." He pauses for breath after saying everything in a rush, and I tilt my head the other way, wondering what's got into him.

"Ah, thank you? You didn't have to do that, Gunnar. I was going to call the plumber this week."

He nods and glances out the doorway. "Now you don't have to," he says with a shrug.

"You're acting nervous," I say when an uncomfortable feeling niggles at my insides. "What did you do?"

"Something I don't want you to get mad about."

"What did you do?" I repeat more firmly.

"I let Maggie feed Viv," he blurts out, ducking his head like I might hit him.

I narrow my gaze at him. Why is he being weird? Does he think I'll be disappointed he didn't do it himself? Viv probably just felt more familiar taking a bottle from a woman. "Why would I get mad about that?"

"With her tits," he adds, cringing.

Oh. There it is. "You *what*?"

He throws up his palms, as if I'm an oncoming freight train he intends to stops with his bare hands. "Viv was screaming and hungry, and she refused the bottle when it had formula. Just flat-out refused. And when I snuck it into her like a dream feed, she woke up and screamed until she vomited, and then she screamed some more, and she was so hungry, and I was desperate, and people used to do it all the time in the old days with wet nurses, and such.

"My aunt breastfed my sister sometimes, when Mom was in no state to do it, and there was no food she could eat, and I didn't know what else to do. We didn't have baby bottles or a store nearby or money... And on the farm, we used the same sort of surrogate methods with orphaned calves or lambs. I know you probably think I'm some dumb back-country guy with weird ideas, but I know some shit, and I swear it was the best option at the time. She was so upset, and she was fucking starving, and it was breaking my heart not to help her, and Maggie had milk, and I just..."

He's practically hysterical, and I can sort of understand why he did what he did, but it feels weirdly like a betrayal.

I watch Viv's cheeks chugging happily, and sigh. She's definitely a boob-girl. "If this *Maggie* woman was kind enough to share her baby's milk with Viv in her time of need, then I suppose I can be grateful. I doubt it was a picnic for her to feed two at once and... *Wait*. You made it sound like they had no kids. They already have a baby?"

Gunnar pales slightly, and his eyes get shifty.

"What is it?" I growl.

"Um... They don't have a baby. Maggie and Ben... He uh... They brought in her milk without..."

"What? *Why?*"

Gunnar glances at my tits, and then closes his eyes. "Some couples enjoy... milk-related activities."

My nipples tingle at the husky gravel tone in his voice, and I know exactly what he's meaning, because I loved the look on his face when I milked myself in front of him, and I have fantasized about him hungry for my breasts more than a few times.

"He milks her for a *sex* thing? And you let her feed our baby?" My voice is so high and pitchy I don't recognize it, and even Viv stops feeding to stare at me in concern, her lower lip pouting. I soothe her and calm myself so she'll settle back at my breast.

"Viv demanded breastmilk, and Maggie had it. She was so hungry, and it was the best I could do for her," he says in a whisper.

"What if Maggie had filthy diseases?" I demand to know.

Gunnar frowns. "She's not some dirty stranger off the street, Jem. She's Ben's girl, and that makes her family. He's the kind of guy who makes sure his girl is in good health. I'd trust that man with my life and Viv's. Maggie feeding Viv was no different to my aunt's feeding my hungry sister when Mom couldn't. Was *that* filthy?" His nostrils are flaring with each breath. "I'd never put Vivvy at risk. *Ever*," he growls, as if I hit a soft spot.

Good. I feel soft all over right now, and to know that he can be wounded too is like justice.

"How can you be sure? Did you have Maggie test-
ed?" I ask.

"She doesn't have diseases," he says, hand on his
heart.

"Oh," I say with a nod. "That's right. She's *sweet and
loving*. I forgot."

Gunnar stalls. His eyes get all squinty at me, and
then he looks at me side-on. "It wasn't like that, Jem." He
opens his mouth to say something else, but wisely closes it
again.

"Can you go, now?" I ask, trying to wrap my head
around things. "I don't want to look at you for a while."

GUNNAR

I was expecting Jem to take more time to cool down, but she lets me come over again the next day.

"I overreacted," she says and hands me Viv, so she can pick up some toys from the floor and put them away in the toy chest I made for them. "I thought about it, and considering how distressed you were when you told me, I can only imagine how you felt when Viv was raging with hunger. It's a heartbreaking situation you've had to face before, and you used your knowledge and experience, to do what was best for Viv with what you had. You gave her what she needed, and I shouldn't get carried away with the finer details, because she's happy and healthy and shared feeding *is* what used to happen. Wet nurses have always existed. And I thought about what I said, too, and how it may have been perceived. I didn't mean to insinuate that what your aunt did was wrong or dirty or would've given your baby sister diseases or anything like that." She gives me a small smile. "I'm sorry if it sounded that way."

I rub at my head and snuggle Viv closer. Astounded by Jem's maturity and the conclusions she drew, as to my emotional upheaval, I'm not sure what to expect next. Is Jason right? Are the young people today more in touch with emotional intelligence? Our generation is so used to grinning and bearing whatever gets thrown at us that I had no idea she'd read into my actions so deeply as to recognize my fucking trauma of being unable to provide for my family. I feel kind of naked.

"Your sister was a little baby when your dad left?" she asks softly.

I nod, at a loss for what is happening. "She could eat some mush, but she was still on the tit," I say before remembering myself with a groan. "*Breastfed*. She wasn't much older than Viv is now." I clear my throat and jiggle my precious girl as I look around. "May I sit for a second?"

Jem raises her eyebrows, stands next to the table, and pushes out one of the dining chairs for me with her foot, the way I had when she'd asked to sit with me in the bar all those months ago. "*Sit*."

I give her a knowing smile, as I take a seat. "Am I a fucking dog?"

"Maybe. Seems like you're pretty obedient, when you want to be." She twists her lips to one side, as she considers me, and I want to realign them, and then plunder her smart fucking mouth. She may be young, but she's not a pushover. She's sassy as fuck, while also being a sweet, caring little mama, and it's a combo I can't get enough of.

"A dog that needs more training, maybe," she says.

"Pretty sure there's a saying about teaching an old dog new tricks, though," she adds with a sigh. "I'm glad you were honest enough to tell me about Maggie, feeding Viv. Okay?"

I nod, and she takes the seat next to mine. "How old were you when your dad left?"

"Eight," I whisper, not sure what she wants the information for, but wanting to give her more honesty.

"Eight?" She looks me over with renewed interest. "That must have been really hard, Gunnar."

"I managed," I say with a frown. "There were good days. Sometimes my aunt could come down with my little cousin and help, like I said. When her man would let her. He wasn't great. But the neighbor was kind. And my guys rallied — Ben, and Jase. Vince, and Daryl...

"Their parents would pack extra into their school lunches, to make sure I was eating. If there was cake, I'd sneak it home for mom. She liked cake, and I liked seeing her smile. I learned how to take care of my family better because people would care for me, and..." I shake my head and stand back up. "I don't want to talk about this stuff, Jem. How the fuck do you make me talk so fucking much? Just leave it alone."

"So... what?" She gives me an unimpressed look. "You're allowed to care about me, but I'm not allowed to care about you? That logic is fucked up, Gunnar Scott. You're my kid's dad. I'm allowed to give a shit. Go sit your ass in the living room and get comfortable."

I hold Viv close and stare at the feisty little miss bossing me around. "I don't know what's happening, and I don't like it," I say.

"Is that an old-dog response to a command?" She rolls her eyes, and gestures at her tits. "I have to feed Viv, and I want to be comfortable while she's drinking. With all the extra milk I brought in through pumping, I have a lot to spare, and I was going to express from the other side while I do it. I'm going to train Viv to be better with a bottle, so it'll be easier for you to feed her. If you're interested."

"Of course I'm interested." I'm already heading for the living room to find a seat and settle in for the show. "I'd love to be able to feed her."

"Good." Jem stands in the doorway to the living room, swinging her manual breast pump and attached bottle like a gunslinger from the wild west. "Because I've decided I want to start getting out more, and I was hoping you'd watch Viv while I do it."

Something in her tone makes me uneasy. What does she mean by *getting out more*? Errands? Dates?

She collects the baby from my arms and sits on the couch next to me. Near enough that I get a seriously close-up view, as she lifts her shirt, unhooks her maternity bra, and latches Viv onto her breast. There is zero shyness involved, and the unguarded sound she makes when the letdown hits sounds like fucking magic in my ears. Every other thought leaves my mind as I soak up the fantasy unfolding before me.

"I've never pumped at the same time as feeding her, so this might get a bit awkward," she says, juggling the pump, while she moves Viv into a different position so she can access her other breast more easily.

Again, she doesn't bother with modesty when she

releases her other, full breast from her bra. It rests there in the open, gloriously round and firm and full of milk. Pale blue-green veins streak her breast, not far below the surface, and I want to spread my palm over them, to see how much of her I can hold and if I can feel her heart beating beneath my fingers.

I swallow hard and try not to stare, but it's hard. It's so fucking hard — much like my dick.

"Can you hold this for a sec, Gun?"

"Mm?"

I lift my focus to the breast pump in her hand. "Sure." I take it and make sure it's all screwed together tight, to ensure the seals are ready for maximum suction. I give the squeeze-trigger a few pumps, and then watch Jem shifting about as if she's trying to get comfortable. "What do you need, little mama? A cushion?" I pass her one, and she accepts it with a smile.

Her bare breasts are fully exposed, and they jostle about as she wriggles on her ass, checks Viv, and then leans back with apparent satisfaction, having found a good position.

Her bare, pale flesh and dark, thick nipple are calling to me in ways that make my mouth water.

Does she even know what she's doing to me?

She strokes her fingertips down the side of her breast as I stare, and she clears her throat. "Do you want to help me get it situated?" She holds her breast, for me to attach the pump.

I stare at her. "What are you doing, Jem?"

"Well, I'm pretty confused by a lot of things, Gunnar, so right now I'm just doing whatever I feel like, to see what happens. What are *you* doing?" Her eyes prompt me to make a decision. She's tempting me.

And I'm so fucking weak around her.

I can be an extra set of hands, to help her here, while restraining myself from doing anything more. Can't I? I suck at my lower lip and set the suction cup against her firm breast, watching her face when I squeeze the trigger a few times, to form an attachment.

Jem utters a soft gasp and shakes her head, as she pushes me and the breast pump away. "I'm too full. I need to milk the breast a little, to get the best seal."

"Do you need an extra hand for that?" I hope she'll say *yes*.

"Or a mouth," she says, looking at Viv. "Sometimes it helps if Viv—"

I lean in, latch on, and suckle at her warm, sweet-smelling breast, gently at first, and then harder.

Jem whimpers, and a rush of warm, watery sweetness gushes into my mouth.

I swallow it down with a beastly, guttural moan. I feel like a fucking animal, but I can't stop. I tug and swallow, tug and swallow, and then finally command myself to pull back, fit the pump to her breast, and work it, to give her the kind of fast, strong suction that leaves her wide eyed and short of breath.

"That better, Miss?" I ask

Panting softly, she nods, and I lower my attention to the flow from her teat, hypnotized by the sight of her milk, spraying from different parts of her nipple. It's satisfying as fuck.

"Won't your girlfriend care that you just did that to me?" she challenges.

With a groan, I drag my hand down my face. "I don't know, but I'm sure your fucking dad will," I say, forcing myself to get off the couch.

My cock is now in Jem's direct line of sight, and I shove my hand inside my jeans, to rearrange where it's pointing and give it a few consolation strokes. "Are you being a deliberate cocktease, Little Miss?"

"Maybe. What are you going to do about it, Daddy? Spank me?" Her eyes sparkle with a challenge, but I can't rise to it.

I shake my head. "The moment I pull down your pants to tan your hide, I'll want to fuck your pretty ass, and I can't do that, Jem. I swore I'd leave your sweet young pussy alone. I'm not renegotiating with your dad any time soon, either. You're still too fucking young, for me to corrupt you. You don't even want a relationship with me. And I told you I was seeing someone. Why are we playing these games?"

"Because you confuse me, and you piss me off, and it makes me feel good and pretty and powerful to make your dick hard," she says with a frown. "But I didn't ask you to suck on my tit just now, so don't blame me for the game you're playing. Also, it'd be great if you could stop acting like I'm a sure thing and that all you need is my dad's blessing. You'd do well to remember that I'm an independent woman, with a mind of my own, and the only person you need permission from to fuck me, is *me*. You're acting like you could have this anytime you want."

She gestures up and down her body. "But I'm off limits to you because *I* say I'm off limits."

I stare at her, so fucking impressed by her strength. She's basically telling me to fuck off, and my dick is straining in my hand so bad I have to choke it, to keep it from bucking around.

She leans back against the couch and looks me over me. "Are you just going to stand there, holding your dick, while I feed your daughter?"

"If I said *yes*, what would you do?" I ask, insanely aroused by her moxie and her milky tits and the way she cares and provides for my baby.

She lifts one shoulder. "I'll lose more respect for you, probably. You talk a big game about me, being too young for you, but I clearly turn you on, and I think you're uncomfortable with how much. Probably because you seem to forget about the woman you're seeing. Remember her?"

I retreat further at her annoyed expression. I do keep forgetting to act like my fake girlfriend is real, and she's right. My behavior is something a shitty boyfriend would do, and that's not the impression I want her to have of me.

"Stop messing with me, Gunnar," Jem says firmly. "It's shitty and confusing, and I'm not interested in being your plaything."

She's laying down the law — the law I should already be following, but it's so fucking hard to leave her be.

I will, though. It's what she's telling me she wants.

I concede with a grunt and pull my hand out of my pants with a smile. "I'm weirdly proud of you, for putting me in my place today, you fierce little fuck."

"Like I need your approval," she says, smirking back. "What are your plans for the rest of the day? Sticking around for some more punishment?"

"Nah. I came to see Viv, but she's fallen asleep on the tit, and apparently her mom wants me to quit staring. Would it be okay if I came back tomorrow?"

"Sure," she says, before sitting up straighter. "In fact, it'd be great if you could watch her tomorrow night, while I go out. I have a date."

My heart shrivels in my chest. "Oh yeah? With who?"

"Someone closer to my age, not that it's any of your fucking business." Her tone is moody and defensive. "You won't mind, will you? Or are you going on a date of your own?"

Will her believing the ruse that I'm fucking another women make her more likely to fuck her date tomorrow?

Ugh. I feel sick. And I have no fucking reason to, because she has every right to do as she pleases — like she said.

As much as I wish things were different, she's not actually mine, and I shouldn't act like she is.

"I'll be alone tomorrow," I say with a tight smile. "You want me to take Viv overnight, so you can bring your date back here?"

"Oh." Jem frowns slightly. "Could you? That'd be amazing. I haven't been laid in forever, and I'm feeling pretty horny, after your mouth was tugging on me. I definitely need to go out and find some cock to ride."

I swallow hard and force a smile. "I don't mind at all.

You're grown woman with needs, and you can satisfy those any way you like, as you well know. I'll see you tomorrow."

G unnar Scott might have a girlfriend, but he's definitely obsessed with my milky tits.

He doesn't pursue his obvious interest, and I have no desire to be *the other woman*, but I do enjoy his appreciative glances and my daydreams, in which we explore the fetish. Whenever I breastfeed around him, he does his best to avert his eyes and hide his hard dick, and when I intentionally test his resolve, I can tell from the tension in his jaw and the string seams of his jeans that he's fucking pining for me. I just don't know what to do with that information.

I may be pining for him too.

He diligently provides everything Viv and I could need, and he's polite and civil, and he does what I want every time I ask — including keeping his sexual advances to himself. Since I told him to stop confusing me, he's basically stopped giving me any of the extra attention he had been.

I miss it.

I didn't think I would, and I appreciate the way he prioritizes our odd little family's needs above all else, but his *Doting Daddy* vibes pull me into a needy spin every time he's near, and I find myself constantly wanting more from him. I miss his heated gazes, and I ache for his touch. He's surrounded me with love and kindness without pressing for more, but I want to feel his love against my skin.

It's unsettling

I thought being alone would be easier, but Gunnar's helping me create the family I always wanted, and by doing so, he makes me dream of a life different from the one I thought would be best for me.

He confuses me even when he's doing his best not to. Why is it so seductive to be cared for? He's helped me stitch my shredded life back together, making the seams stronger so I can count on them to hold.

Dad and Gabe have recommitted to each other, and they're stable. They're each other's best medicine, it seems, and I'm grateful I don't have to worry about them. It's a real load off my mind.

They're pretty good with Viv, and I know they love me, but our relationship may never fully heal. They're not as interested in my life as they are in each other, which is fine, but I've gone from being essential to the running of the family, to being sort of unnecessary.

It's like I got so good at looking after myself that nobody thinks to check in with me, to see if I need any support.

Except Gunnar.

And I've been fake-dating people, to keep him at a

distance, while also hoping to make him jealous — which is stupid when he's dating someone else. I just want him to believe I'm sought after. I want him to think other people desire and love me, but the truth is, nobody really does. Not the way I'd like them to. Nobody makes me feel wanted the way he does.

I thought no strings was the best option.

But a heart without strings is a lonely thing.

I didn't want to give my heart away, when the people I've loved have only broken it, but if I think about it, Gunnar gave me back both of my dads. If he hadn't stepped in to say something and shown me how to hold my fathers accountable, where would I be right now? Still struggling to take care of Viv and my Dad and my career. Something was going to have to give, but with Gunnar involved, I didn't have to give up anything. Everything got easier. And *better*.

He's calm and steady, and he listens like he's actually interested in the things I say. And even though I told him I didn't want him, he keeps showing up each day, to love his daughter and support her mom.

I feel loved by him.

More so than by anyone else.

And despite my efforts not to, I think I love him too.

My heart wants Gunnar Scott to wrap me in his big arms while he asks to *watch the latest TikToks*, so he can chuckle at my little critters having picnics and tell me I should be on kids' afternoon TV. That it'd be cool if Viv could watch them from the couch when she's older, and he could sit beside her, eating their afternoon snacks, while they giggle at Mama's silly voices.

When I imagine that, I want to fill the couch with enough kids that they're climbing on him, so he can't get up. Not that he'd want to. In my head, he'd love our family to grow big and happy too. He wants a home filled with so much love, our kids will never doubt that they're cared for and treasured.

And I want to giggle with him under the bedcovers, while we watch the little adult versions of those woolly-critter videos I've made just for him. I've actually spent the last two months crocheting and filming a few. It's sort of what I do on my *dates*.

Shelby points to my knitting bag near the door, on her way into the kitchen. "As handy as it is for me that Gunnar's agreed to babysit Jaxon while he's here watching Viv tonight, I'd happily forgo my plans and babysit for you two, so you can fuck out all that sexual tension you're both carrying around," she says with a smirk. "Why don't you tell him you want to date him, instead of going on pretend adult playdates?"

I pull a face at Viv and sigh. "He's with someone else, Shelby."

"Well, maybe he's seeing her because he's lonely and you said he can't be with you. From what I can tell, he's crazy about you and Viv. Have you not seen the way he looks at you? Do you not hear how he talks about you? He sounds like a smitten, protective, action-figure-y hero with a crush the size of Texas. I've never even heard him talk about that other woman. Have you met her? Is it serious or more of a casual thing?"

"I don't know." I wipe my palms on my jeans. "It's not serious enough to talk sperm with her."

Shelby tosses her hair back and laughs. "*What?*"

I shake my head. "Nothing. You think he'd consider dating me instead, if I asked?"

"What do you have to lose? If he says no, you can always get your dick fix somewhere else." She waves a dismissive hand in the air. "You're more than welcome to come out dancing with me, if he turns you down." She does a spin in her slinky dress and shimmies her tits at me. "My closet is all yours if you want to go change." She looks me up and down and shakes her head. "Who do you think Gunnar believes you're meeting when you wear jeans and a T-shirt on your dates?"

I look down at my tight, cropped *Metallica* Tee. "It's a sexy T-shirt."

"Uh-huh," she says, nodding. "I just feel like he'd rather see more cleavage. That man stares at your tits like he wants to latch on when you're not looking."

My cheeks warm, because I immediately think of the way he did do just that, and how fucking good it felt. I glance down at my T-shirt again. "The man does like tits," I agree. "And he was at the farm for Ben and Maggie's wedding over the weekend, so he'll probably be all about the tits tonight."

"Why's that?" Shelby asks.

I shouldn't have said anything. I don't want to tell her Gunnar's got a kinky lactation infatuation. I'm pretty sure that grown men, being excited about breastfeeding, isn't meant to be as fucking hot as my wet-pussy response claims it is, and I don't want her to think Gunnar's a freak, because that would make me a freak, too.

"Well, he hasn't seen these things for a few days, and

I'm hoping he's had withdrawals," I explain, gesturing to my tits before I groan. "Why do I hope that, Shelby? Why do I want him to see me and be so overwhelmed with need he'll take me on the spot in a way that'll make Viv a little brother or sister?" I lower my head to my hands. "What's wrong with me?"

"My diagnosis? Semen deficiency," Shelby says with a grin. "I hear there's an injection for that. Maybe you should get it tonight. I'm sure Gunnar has some in stock for you."

My brain grabs the idea and runs with it, and the fantasy is enough to make me squeak. It brings with it a great sense of urgency to tell him what I want — love and more babies. Can I be that bold? Maybe. If I looked the part.

I hold Viv out toward Shelby. "Would you watch Viv, while I run up and change?"

"I was hoping you'd ask," Shelby says as she takes the baby. "We'll go play in the living room with Jax, until your hunky babysitter arrives."

"He's not her babysitter; he's her dad," I correct her and rush upstairs, to put on the dress I wore the night Gunnar made Viv with me.

I shiver as I slip into it, forgoing underwear again. It may feel a little silly if he ignores me and I spend the rest of my evening sitting in my car, knitting, but it's worth the risk when the alternative may be him, choosing to be with me, spreading me wide, pinning me down with his mouth on my tits, and fucking me bare until I'm pregnant with another of his babies.

Another thrill runs through me.

He likes to be in charge, but he also likes it when I speak my mind.

Am I brave enough to tell him I'm not confused anymore? That I want him? That I want him to want me? That I want our family to grow?

What if he says, *Aw, that's cute, Little Miss, but Daddy's with a big girl now, and she always knows what she wants*? Am I strong enough to risk that rejection?

The doorbell rings, and I hurry to put on some mascara and lip gloss, so I look like I'm trying.

I walk down the stairs slowly, meeting Gunnar's gaze when he looks up.

His eyes widen, and he swears under his breath. Shelby giggles as she lifts his arm, sets Viv against his chest, and wraps his arm back around the baby tightly.

With apparent difficulty, he tears his gaze from me and greets his daughter. "Hey, Viviana Bea. Your mama's looking pretty fancy tonight." He glances at me again and closes his eyes, seeming kind of nervous as he scrapes his hand through his hair and rubs the back of his neck.

"Um..." He squeezes his eyes shut tighter and then opens them to glance at Shelby, and then at Viv. "Shelby, could you please take Viv back, for a sec? I was hoping to talk to Jem for a bit. In private."

Shelby graciously does as he asked, turning so she can make an *ooh, the sexy dress worked* kind of face at me with kissy-lips and wiggling eyebrows, where he can't see her.

"Could we step outside, Jem?" he asks, regaining my attention.

I nod, follow him out onto the front steps, and close the door behind us.

"You look beautiful." He takes a long, indulgent look, and then swallows visibly.

"Is that what you wanted to tell me?" I ask with a smile.

He shakes his head, and his nervous energy comes back threefold. It's worse than the time he told me he let Maggie breastfeed Viv.

"I... Oh, this is hard," he says, wiping his brow.

My stomach drops. "Are you getting married?" I ask, my mind rushing to connect his behavior with his actions.

He frowns. "What? *No.* Why would you think that? I'm not even seeing anyone."

"You're not?" I ask, confused.

He groans softly and pulls at his hair. "I'm just going to say it," he says, restless on his feet.

My stomach begins to knot with nerves, but not the good kind. "Say what?" I whisper.

"Ben and Maggie got married, and I told you we were all helping them get pregnant, because they can't afford IVF. Right?"

My frown deepens. "Uh huh."

"The thing is, it wasn't working when Ben used our samples to inseminate her artificially, so we all..." Gunnar closes his eyes and looks as if he's bracing for impact. "I fucked her. We all did. At the same time. Well, one after the other, but—" He shakes his head and balls his fists like he wants to punch himself, and I'm almost disappointed when he doesn't.

"I feel awful about it," he declares, meeting my eyes

with visible levels of shame and remorse. "Not about helping my friends," he clarifies, "but because the whole time I was helping them and doing this thing, I was pretending it was you. I was imagining it was you I was breeding, and I wanted it so badly to be true. But it wasn't you, and I feel so fucking guilty."

I stare at him, too stunned to move or speak.

"I'm not doing it again," he states firmly. "I want you to know that. They can have my seed, but I can't do that again. I can't keep burying my emotions and denying what I feel for you anymore, Jem. It's making me fucking crazy, and I can't get through the day without my need for you making every fucking moment torturous because I can't be with you."

Huh? Am I meant to be angry, shocked, or wooed right now? He's saying shit I hate at the same time as things I want to hear, and my insides are going haywire.

"I want you, Little Miss," he says, his voice dropping deeper. "I know you know that, and I know you don't want it. I know you're enjoying your freedoms and going out, fucking other guys, and that's fine. I get it. You're young, and I was your first, and you didn't intend for me to be hanging around like I do. You wanted no strings. But I want the fucking strings, Jem. I want you and Viv and a family. I want to fucking marry you, and take care of you, and support you, and fuck your smart little brains out every fucking night. I love you. And I'm sick of pretending I don't."

He loves me? It's what I wanted to hear, but why am I hearing it like this? Mixed with a bunch of shit I really don't want to fucking know.

My vision blurs. How fast can my heart beat before I pass out? Why can't I breathe?

"I *like* that you're younger than me," Gunnar continues, bombarding me with a confession that makes me whimper and squeeze my thighs together, to smother the inappropriate ache. My body adores that aspect of our relationship too, but I don't want to admit that right now.

"I know I shouldn't be so turned on by such a massive age gap," he says with a shrug as he pales. "That it makes me a sick fuck, who preys on your innocent fucking soul, but I like your sweet face and savvy, modern sense of the world. I like that I can't stop thinking about you — that I haven't stopped thinking about you from the night we met."

My mind can't make sense of his words. It's chaos inside my head, and I feel like I'm frozen in the center, too stunned to react. What is he saying?

"It's been more than a year since our night together, and I haven't fucked a single woman since then, Jem — besides Maggie, this weekend. And that was nothing to do with wanting to be with her. She's Ben's. And I'm not interested. I only want for you — would have you be mine, if only you wanted it too. And I know you probably want me even less now than you did before, and that you're dating other people... *God*, that fucking kills me. But you said it was what you needed, so I support you when you go out looking all fucking sexy in your jeans and sneakers and those tiny, cute fucking T-shirts that make me want to—"

He looks me over again and moans. "This outfit is a whole different thing, and after what happened when you wore this dress around me, I'm scared of where you're going tonight, and what you'll do in it, but that's not why I'm telling you this. I'm not trying to stop you from living your life and having fun. I don't ever want that. I want to be part of it, and I'll respect your boundaries and follow your lead. I just want you to know that I think you're a wonderful mother and the sexiest little smart-mouthed fuck I've ever met, and that making a family with you would be so fucking nice. I'd be your guy and take care of everyone. When you're ready for more kids, I want you to ask me if I'll make them with you, Jem. I just..."

My jaw drops and he winces.

He nods his head slowly. Sadly. "You don't want that. You're young, and your career is going to be so fucking big, and women get so much pressure to do it all. I want to help you do it all, and you keep telling me you don't need me, but it doesn't stop me from wanting you to.

"You're going to be amazing, Jem. I mean, you already are, but the rest of the world is going to eat you up, because you're that fucking delicious. I'd totally take care of all your babies, so you could shine. Even if they're not mine."

What?

I narrow my eyes at him. "You'd help me raise some other guy's kids?"

Gunnar face remains earnest as he shrugs. "They'd be Viv's siblings, and I'd be amicable. More than amicable, because I fucking care. You don't need drama, and I only want there to be love in your home. You deserve that. And I'll do whatever you need me to, because I fucking love you, Jemma Wade."

My heart stutters, and I feel around for something to hold, to keep myself upright.

He steps closer. "I love you, and if you want to cancel your date tonight, to go on one with me instead, I'd be the happiest man alive. I'll march next door and tell your dads they have to watch the kids until tomorrow, because I'm going to need to give you my full attention all fucking night, and then some. I'll love you forever, if you'll fucking let me." He's breathing hard, and his eyes are glistening as if he's on the verge of tears. He means every fucking word.

I lean back against the door, trying to find my bearings after having so much intensity hurled at me in such a short amount of time. I need to digest. I think aloud, hoping to better understand all he's said.

"You took me outside to... tell me you gang-banged Ben's milky wife, that you lied to me about having a girlfriend because you *love* me, and you haven't fucked anyone else in a *year*?"

"It's been more than a year. Until this weekend." As he adds the last part, he sinks to his knees. "And that just proved to me that I was right to abstain. I only want you, Jem. But I'll understand if you need me to continue keeping my distance. You requested no strings, and I've made a right fucking Gordian knot of things."

I snort. I don't know if I've heard anyone use *Gordian knot* in a conversation before, but Gunnar Scott often surprises me with the depth of his thinking. Does working with stone give him the kind of silence he needs for that level of contemplation? Is that why he likes it?

"We've both made a tangle of this," I say with a sigh, nudging him with my toes. "Get up and come inside."

"Are you mad at me?" he asks.

"Definitely," I reply without pause.

He nods and keeps his gaze low. "Okay. I didn't want that, but I understand. Will you...?" He lifts his gaze to my dress for a moment before his shoulders sink lower. "If you need to stay out later, let me know. I can sleep on your couch, or I can take the kids back to my place, if you decide to bring someone back with you. I—" He shakes his head. "Take good care of yourself, Jem. It'd ease my mind some if you could be sure he'll treat you well." He closes his eyes with a sigh. "Easing my mind is probably pretty low on your priorities right now, but just... Don't settle for less than you deserve."

"Are you telling me what to do?" I ask, half-patronized and half-flattered he cares, but one-hundred-percent sure I don't need his approval.

He shakes his head again, his gaze sincere. "I just want you to be happy and safe."

"Great." I go inside to kiss Viv *goodbye*. "Come on, Shelby. We've got dancing and men to do."

"We do?" She looks between me and Gunnar, as I drag her toward the door. "Oh. Yeah. We definitely do. Thanks for babysitting, Gunnar."

Eager to put distance between myself and the man who's overwhelming me, I pull Shelby out the door in a hurry and head for the car.

SHELBY STARES at me across the table.

"Wait. *What?* Him and his bros got it on with their friend's wife — with the guy's permission — to help them conceive? *Wow.* That is some redneck shit, right there." She giggles and sips her drink. "Goes with the territory, though. The guy's from the back country mountains of fuck-knows-where, so it's not surprising they'd do shit *the old-fashioned way.* Are you mad? You seem mad."

I poke at the ice floating in my soda. "I don't know what I am. I think I'm confused again. He was all awkward, like it was some big confession because he felt guilty."

"Guilty for what? Fucking another woman? You already knew he was fucking someone else. And this baby-making thing for his friend doesn't sound like he's in love with the woman or anything."

"He's not," I agree. "He's in love with me. He said so."

Shelby slams down her glass and leans in. "He did?"

I nod. "And he's not fucking anyone else. He said he hasn't fucked anyone since we met, apart from this thing he did with his friends, which he feels awful about and won't ever do again."

"Because he loves you," Shelby says, staring at me.

I nod again. "He said he loves me and wants to be together. He wants to make babies with me and take care of us all forever," I say in a rush, petrified of how much I want that. "That he'll support me any way I need him to, so I'll get everything I want and won't have to sacrifice anything or set my career goals aside."

Shelby looks thoughtful a moment before she nods. "He doesn't talk with me a lot, but I don't think I've had a single conversation with him where he hasn't smiled when he says your name. And if there's any mention of parenting, knitting, or TikTok, he cannot stop gushing about how fucking talented you are — and rightfully so, I might add."

I blush and give her a lop-sided shrug. "He also said a bunch of other really sweet shit. The kind of things he'd only say if he really fucking loved me and has thought about it hard enough to make peace with the idea of rejection if I tell him I don't intend to love him back. Really brave shit, Shelby. Like how he'll keep supporting me as best he can, even if I move on and it means helping to raise another man's kids as Viv's siblings and stuff."

She stares at me. "That's some deep love and commitment, Jem."

"I know," I whisper.

"Do you believe him?" she asks. "He's not just saying what he thinks you want to hear? He'd actually make good on his promises?"

Every part of me has faith that he would. I press my lips together and nod.

"So, why are you still sitting here?" she asks, searching my face. "Earlier you were excited by the thought of being with him and making more babies, and the man just told you he wants the same thing and that you have his heart by the balls. Do you want the guy or not?"

I run my palms up and down my thighs. "I want him more than I want to."

Shelby's perplexed expression remains fixed in place. "I don't know what that means."

"I don't like wanting him so much," I paraphrase. "It makes me feel... vulnerable."

"That's the fear talking. You don't listen to that. You trust what your heart says."

"But fear talks louder," I argue.

Shelby rolls her eyes. "So your heart says, *Go home and fuck him*, then?"

I give her a pained look. "My head says it won't work out. He makes me sound like I'm some amazing catch, but I'm not that lovable. Even my own parents aren't that interested in me."

Shelby stills. "Look, Jem. You've been through a lot, and I can understand why you may not want to trust in love," she says calmly, "but you have a legitimate chance to create the kind of family you want with the seriously hot and adorably caring man you crave, and you're finding excuses to not to be happy. You're being a chicken-shit little bitch, and as your friend, it's my duty to point that out, in case you can't see it. If you're feeling vulnerable, you go home to Gunnar and demand that he loves you in a way that makes you feel strong."

"He already does." I fidget with the hem of my borrowed dress. "That's why I love him so much."

Shelby gives me a flat stare, then picks up my soda and tips it down my front.

I leap off my chair, and when I finally stop squealing

and dancing around from all the ice that went down my low-cut dress, I glare at her.

"You need to go home," she says with a serene smile. "You'll thank me in the morning."

I lift my chin, and try to act dignified as I stand dripping on the barroom floor. "Well played, Shelby Cooper." I give her a shallow bow and collect my purse. "I hate you for doing that, but I know you're right. Thank you."

GUNNAR

Jem's front door opens and closes, while I'm stuck on the couch, boxed in by sleeping babies. I don't want to move and risk waking them when they've only just drifted off, so I crane my neck to see if it's Jem or Shelby.

Please be Jem. Just Jem. And no stupid asshole. Not when I can't yet escape from my position. I'll be forced to listen to him fucking her upstairs while I'm covering the kid's ears so they don't wake up crying from the noises Jem makes... if he can even make her scream the right way.

If he makes her scream the wrong way, I'll be up those fucking stairs so fast, he won't know what hit him.

My right hand automatically curls into a fist, and when Jem comes into the living room alone, my heart pounds with the need to avenge her, but I'm not yet sure who needs the punishment or what I need to protect her from. She looks... wet? But it's not raining out. Her eyes are red and puffy, and she has a lost-little-girl look on her face that makes me want to wrap her into my arms and make her feel better.

"What happened?" I ask in a gentle voice, even though I feel very ready to inflict pain on whomever upset her. "Are you okay?"

The need to be on my feet and at her side is hard to curb, but my arms are full of babies. I try to lay Jaxon on the couch with one arm, doing my best not to wake him or disturb Viv who's nearly sound asleep in the crook of my other arm.

They both stir and suckle at their bottle teats but stay peaceful, and I fence them in with pillows tucked tight against them, to keep them from rolling off the couch in their sleep.

I check to make sure they're safe, and then rise from my crouch and turn to Jem.

She's staring at me with her big blue eyes full of fear.

"What's wrong, beautiful?" I ask in my softest whisper. "Why do you look so scared?" I rub at my chest. "Your eyes are making my heart sore. Tell me what's going on."

She lifts her arms above her head and keeps them there, like she's waiting for me to do something. Take off her clothes?

I search her face and look over her wet dress. What horrific event rendered her traumatized, speechless, and in need of my help for this?

I approach slowly, my palms raised. "Okay. I'll take it off."

Slowly, to make sure it's what she wants, I take the hem of her dress in hand and carefully lift it up and over her head, to leave her naked in front of me apart from her sneakers. There's a throw on the nearby armchair, and I carefully wrap it around her.

"Why are you wet and... *sticky*, little mama?" I lean in, to smell her, when she doesn't respond. "Is that *grape soda*?" I ask.

I lean back and study her again. "Who poured a drink over you? What do they look like? Tell me where you were, and I'll go teach them some fucking manners."

Her eyes become even rounder and start to shine with unshed tears, as her chin dimples and her bottom lip quivers.

"I'm sorry," I whisper, pulling her into a hug. "I didn't mean to scare you. I just growl things sometimes. I'm not growling at you. I swear."

"I know," she squeaks. "Will you please put the children to bed?"

I release her slowly. "Of course. You'll be okay? Here, by yourself? You need something before I go? Some water? I'll get you some water."

Her tears brim over, and she nods as she croaks, "I *do* want some water."

Oh fuck, I want to hug her again.

I take a step toward the kitchen and glance at the babies on the couch, and then back at her. "You'll keep an eye on the babies? I tucked 'em in, but I don't want them to fall. Will you watch them, so I know that fierce little mama inside you is in charge? That she's strong enough to handle this room if I leave it? There's nothing scary in here, right?" With a little smile, I add, "Not even me."

Jem gives me a vague nod and a twitch of her lips that could be a smile if it didn't make her look so nervous.

I think about that, while I get her a glass of water and put Jaxon into his crib, upstairs, in Shelby's room. I come back down and pick up Viv. Snuggling her close and kissing her forehead, I sneak away the almost empty bottle of breastmilk she's been dream-suckling on. "Daddoo loves you, Sweet Pea. I gotta go home while you're sleeping, but I'm coming back, I promise."

I turn to offer Jem a chance to say *goodnight*, but she stiffens when I face her. Her eyes are all big again, like those of a critter caught in the headlights.

I point at myself and frown. "Am *I* what scares you?"

She lifts one shoulder and focuses on Viv before edging closer. She kisses Viv's curls, whispers her good-night wishes, and then returns her gaze to me, like I might do something bad.

"I don't want to be someone who bothers you, Jem," I say. "I'm going to put Viv to bed, and then I'll get out of your hair if you don't need me. Okay? You want me to turn on the shower, to warm it up for you, while I'm up there?"

Jem's nose twitches, and she almost rolls her eyes before shaking her head. *No.*

"Right. You just want me gone. I can do that," I say with a nod, feeling like a fucking rock in her shoe. "I'll be done in a minute"

Jem's still standing in the same spot when I come back down, and she looks right at me before dropping the throw I wrapped around her.

She stands there, silent and naked and pretty and covered in sticky grape soda, and I don't know what to think.

Why would she act like this?

I point at myself, and then at the door, before raising my eyebrows. *Do you want me to leave?*

She shakes her head.

I take a deep breath and rumble softly in frustration.

She steps one foot forward and taps it on the carpet, like she wants me to stand in front of her. It makes her boobs jiggle, and I want to grip her hard and shake her till her words fall out.

I step into the spot her cute rainbow-painted toes pointed out and lean in close. "You're being very fucking confusing right now, Jemma Wade," I whisper, as I run the tip of my nose across her bare shoulder, testing to see how she'll react to the touch.

She shivers, and her lips part on a soft breath.

I snake out my tongue and flick it along her sticky skin, confirming it *is* grape soda she's wearing. Jem tilts her neck, inviting me to lick her more, and I do. I press my lips to her neck, and then suckle and tease her skin before giving her a nip that draws a louder gasp from her.

"If you don't tell me what the fuck is going on, I'm going to lose my shit and come all over your beautiful fucking body," I whisper near her ear. "I don't think you realize how hard I'm working to keep it together, Little Miss, but I can assure you that my cock is primed and you have my full fucking attention." I move to where I can see her eyes again. "Who threw soda on you?"

"Shelby," she whispers, gazing up at me.

I lean back and scratch at my beard. "Why would she do that? Was it an accident?"

Jem shakes her head. "She did it on purpose."

"Why? She's supposed to be your friend."

"She did it *because* she's my friend."

I squint at her. "I don't get it."

"She sent me home to change." Jem hooks her fingers over my belt, pulls me closer, and strokes my cock through my jeans. "And change is fucking terrifying."

Gunnar studies me, his brow furrowed in concentration. "What do you mean?"

What do I mean?

I mean that I love him beyond fucking measure.

Since I walked in the door, I've seen him snuggled with sleeping babies who trust him to keep them safe. He's so fucking caring and mindful and gentle with them, to protect them from harm, and it makes all my fucking eggs crave fertilization by him. I read somewhere that a woman my age can have hundreds of thousands — that's a lot of eggs. It's a big fucking craving.

Epic Daddoo skills aside, he was just as mindful and gentle with me — was ready to battle my enemies or back off if I needed him to, while letting me know loud and clear that he didn't want to go anywhere and leave me vulnerable and exposed.

He read me like book and licked grape soda from my skin as both temptation and a warning, and I want every single thing he promises. I have all along, but I never fight for what I want because he acts like I'm some great prize, and I'm scared he'll figure out how wrong he is, how not-special and forgettable I am, and how easy it is for people to walk out of my life.

I suck in a deep breath. "Shelby ruined her dress, so I'd have to come home and talk to you. She said I have to stop being a chicken-shit little bitch and tell you how I feel."

I begin to undo his belt buckle, but he clamps his hand over mine, preventing me.

"Attacking my pants isn't telling me how you feel, Jem." He tightens his grip when I try to escape his grasp, and he tilts his head like he means business. "What are you afraid of?"

"Liking you too much," I blurt out, ripping my hand away and folding my arms over my breasts, to feel less exposed.

"What does that mean, *liking me too much?*" He offers me the soft, woolen couch blanket again. "Loving me?"

I take the knitted throw, toss it back on the ground, then press my lips together and give the slightest nod.

"You're afraid to love me?" he asks, searching my face.

I nod again, and he sweeps me into his arms and sits on the couch with me in his lap. "Tell me why. Is it because I'm too old? Too rough? Too ugly? I don't know how to make the TikToks? What is it, Jem? I'm not good enough? Smart enough? I make bad choices? Follow my dick too much and suck your tits when I shouldn't? I'm boring? I don't smell good? Tell me what it is that makes me so hard to love."

I frown. "You're easy to love."

He stares at me a moment, grunts, and then sets me back on my feet. "If that were true, you wouldn't be scared of doing it."

"I don't want to be," I whisper. My eyes are getting hot again.

Gunnar draws his eyebrows down hard and pulls me back into his lap. "Why are you scared, beautiful?"

"Because I don't want my heart to break when you leave me."

"*When* I leave you?" He looks insulted. "You're Jemma Wade. My beautiful, kind, clever, and sassy-as-fuck Little Miss. Mother of my child. Grower-slash-nurturer of my cute-as-a-button wild oat. You're the woman I can't get out of my head — the only fucking fantasy in my spank bank. You're the literal girl of my dreams. I want to go back in time to when you said *no strings* and wrap us up in so much fucking string you can never get us untied. Why would I ever want to fucking *leave* you? I literally said I'd stay yours even if you found someone else and grew a whole new family without me. I wouldn't love knowing someone else was breeding my girl, but I could live with it if you were happy. I'd fucking stay in your life, Jem. I feel like I can't live without you. I love you."

I wipe my eyes. I know he loves me; I feel it every day. It's what makes him so wonderful to be around. "I love you too," I squeak. "But I don't want to end up like Dad did. I don't want to be that sad and have to pick up whatever shitty pieces of my heart are left when you're gone, like I had to when Gabe left and it brought back all the feelings about my mom not wanting me. I don't want to feel that way again, Gunnar."

"You won't have to, because I ain't *leaving*," he growls. He sets me onto the couch and yanks his belt open, and then off. "Am I a good dad, Jem?"

"What?"

"Am. I. A. Good. Father?" he asks in a low, husky voice. "Do I take good care of my kid? Provide for her? Love her? Do whatever she needs me to do? Be who she needs me to be? Do you believe I'll do that forever?"

I nod.

"Right," he says, tearing open the fly of his jeans and pulling out his massive cock. "Then spread your legs, and I'll fuck another baby into you right now. Will that convince you I'll stay? I don't abandon my family like a fucking asshole. I work my ass off and make sure they're taken care of. You know I'll fucking be around for my kids, Jem. And eventually, you'll understand I'm here for you, too. That I'll *keep* being here for you. I love *all* of you."

I stare up at him, and spread my legs so wide there's no mistaking what I want.

Gunnar rumbles. "Look at you, shining that pretty little cunt at me like a good fucking girl," he says before sealing his mouth over mine in a needy, brutish kiss.

He pulls me with him as he stands, and his moan

tastes delicious. Aggressive kisses assail my throat, and his rough palms bring my skin to life when he drags his hands downward to grab my ass. He lifts me from the floor, and I wrap my legs around his waist.

He starts to walk with me toward the stairs, but then turns back and lowers me down onto the couch again. Is it because the kids are sleeping up there and he doesn't want us to wake them when he makes me moan?

I grind against his firm body, ready to get loud, and Gunnar grows more frantic, ripping off his shirt. "Tell me you want my big fucking cock, Little Miss," he pants between kisses.

"I want it, Daddy," I whisper, as his hot lips trail down my chest. I clutch at his thick hair, grateful he hasn't cut it in a while, and slide against his abs, slicking them with my arousal.

"Tell me you want my seed. I can put it anywhere. Fuck you bare and watch you drip."

I rock my hips into him with a grateful sigh. "Yes, Daddy."

"I can breed you hard and stick around, to watch you grow," he growls, grabbing my hair and twisting it in his fist until I hiss and meet his gaze. "Do you know how fucking crushed I was that I missed your first pregnancy?" he asks, the devastation clear on his face before his expression turns pleading. "Tell me I can stay, beautiful."

I nod, gritting my teeth in a growl when it makes my scalp sting.

Gunnar grunts, and lowers his lips to my breast, to kiss softly and then draw my nipple deep into his mouth.

He tugs at me so hard, I cry out and buck, and then he does something incredible with his tongue, like he's snapping the tip of my nipple while he sucks at me. He drinks down my flow with an epic thirst, lighting up my entire body when the letdown hits me with its rush of endorphins.

He keeps sucking, swallowing my milk in greedy gulps. I swear under my breath and thrust my chest higher, needing more of the heady sensation. "*Daddy.*"

He responds beautifully, intensifying his naughty antics.

What the hell is it about this big, bearded man feeding at my breast that makes me feel so wanton? He's working me into a damned frenzy, starting out all gentle in a tease, and then pulling half my fucking tit inside his mouth and sucking at me so hard I want to ride his cock and spray milk down his throat.

His mouth compresses around my breast with every swallow, delivering the most delicious pressure, and he gives a soft, satisfied little grunt or rumble with each mouthful of breastmilk he devours, before suckling again with gusto, begging for more.

It's like he can't get enough, and I may actually feel the same.

When he finally releases me, my nipple is fucking pulsating, and so is my clit.

"More, Daddy. *Please.*" I urge him onward, squeezing my thighs to his sides and rubbing against him, to ease the throbbing need between my legs.

Gunnar latches on to my other breast, his hot mouth quick to pull at me hard and hungry. Every so often, he eases back a little to flick at my nipple with his tongue, and it makes my head feel all floaty. It's fun and completely fucking different from feeding a baby.

He slides his big hands under my ass and grips hard, urging me to grind more firmly. He strokes my gushing pussy and moans into my breast.

My core quivers, and I grab at his head, his ears, anything I get hold of, to bring him closer. Bring him inside.

He teases my asshole with his slippery fingers, and I give a needy whimper when the pressure increases. He pushes inside my tightest hole, stretching, and then slides his thick finger in and out while he sucks and pulls and tugs at my breast, to swallow me down.

"*Daddy*," I beg, panting as he works his way deeper into my ass.

He fucks me there with his big finger, forcing me closer to the edge while I gush arousal to lubricate his work.

My nipple slips from his mouth, and he scuffs his beard along my sensitive skin before gazing down at me with complete infatuation. "Taking Daddy's finger like such a good girl." He rocks his hips, until his cock streaks my skin with pre-cum that quickly cools, to make me shiver.

My pussy twitches at his abs, and I tilt my pelvis every which way to find purchase for the friction I need on my clit, but it evades me, lingering just out of reach until I'm a writhing, pleading, bucking mess with an empty pussy and a full ass. "*Daddy*."

"Soon, Miss. Daddy wants you fucking drenched for his cock."

He latches on to my other breast again, and swivels the finger in my ass so he can spread me wider and get closer. Somehow, he curls, to hollow out his position and make his torso concave, so he can keep feeding at my breast while he presses the lower half of his body close enough for his cock to slide against my slick inner thighs.

A deeply primal moan reverberates through my breast, and he's almost-fucking his hand while its finger pleasures my ass. His curls brush against mine in a gentle kiss, and then a full-blown assault, giving me a new, more targeted pressure on my clit to enjoy. The difference is everything I wanted, and my body instantly pulls tight, ready to snap and unravel.

Gunnar tugs sharply at my breast and uses his controlling presence in my ass to drive me into the firmness beneath his curls, milling my clit hard. It feels so good, I'm going to lose my fucking mind.

He leaves my breast and gives a low, harsh rumble before his husky voice rains down on me like fireworks. "Come, baby girl. Come, and I'll fuck you bare while you shudder and scream."

He pushes at my ass, and my core explodes in a body-wracking quake. I cry out and squirt all over his curls, his cock, and his big, tight balls.

The intense pressure in my ass eases as his finger retreats, and he grips the undersides of my thighs in a fierce hold and growls.

"Yes, Little Miss. Fucking soak me." He wedges his giant cock at the entrance of my clenching pussy, and I cry out when he forces his way inside. He stretches my inner walls, but they squeeze even tighter in pleasure, keeping him from pushing deeper.

"Fucking take it," he commands, shoving deep. He pulls back, and then slams in to the hilt. "There's my good girl."

His praise washes over me in a euphoric haze. I'm stretched and full and instead of feeling pain at his rough penetration, the explosive delight in my core doubles down. It should've hurt, but my pussy is fucking celebrating his aggressive breach, and I'm clamping at his cock like the pleasure won't ever fade.

He thrusts at me hard, pumping his fat cock in and out of my wet cunt, while I wail and twitch and tremble. "So fucking tight," he purrs. "My good, perfect, Little Miss."

I can't stop coming. Or moaning my absolute gratitude with every ragged breath at being made to come so fucking long and hard.

At the mercy of his strength, my body shakes, and I claw at him, grappling for something to hold on to, as the intensity of my orgasm increases. It grips at me, pulling every muscle rigid, and I try to brace for more. But that tension transfers to him through our connection, and I squeeze his cock so hard, he's forced to become even more savage in his thrusts.

He spears into my depths with a vigor that forces my seized-tight pussy to accommodate his massive size, his cock punishing my flesh. "Yes, little mama. Squeeze that pretty little cunt, you beautiful fucking woman."

He gives me no chance to settle, only urges me

onward, until I relinquish all control, to let him transform me into a creature of pure pleasure. Not for the first time, he takes care of my every need, working any resistance from my body until I'm softened clay in his hands — his to mold and shape and please as he sees fit.

The moment I relent in his arms, a pliable captive of his love, his touch becomes gentle and tender. The violence of my climax begins to fade into calmer, blissful waves that rock me into a sated, limp, and dreamy daze.

Gunnar draws me close, buries himself deep inside me, and rumbles low and long and hard. He pulses his seed at my core in powerful spurts I can feel washing over my limits, to sooth my ravaged, jittery flesh. His lips find my neck, and he murmurs sweet words against my sticky skin between tiny, needy licks that he slowly trails to my breast.

He closes his warm lips around my nipple and suckles softly, as he empties himself, filling me to over-flowing. His slow, basting movements begin to squelch in a filthy way that makes my pussy ripple some more, and he hums at my breast before letting my nipple slip from his mouth.

"Mmm..." he hums again, looking down at me with total adoration, while his cock stirs his cum into my flut-tering pussy. "My beautiful girl. I'm going to fucking love you forever. Don't you worry about me stopping. I never fucking will." He seals his lips over mine and steals my breath with a kiss so full of emotion, it brings tears to my eyes.

There's a promise in his every touch, and I want

everything he's offering. His love, his support, his body. All of him. It's for me.

For our family.

He's got me. And he's never letting go.

I surrender to his love, trusting him to keep me and keep me well.

His cock slurps from me as he pulls back, and he lowers his mouth to my clit, to slowly press his tongue over the sensitive node in a lingering lick that makes my pussy tremble.

His cum trickles from within me, and Gunnar smears it over my thighs and up across my belly that still feels a bit gelatinous from having Viv. He spreads me wide and stares at the mess he made of me, a satisfied look on his face.

He shifts his gaze to meet mine and presses his hand to me. The heel of his palm gently mills my clit, and he stretches his fingers upward, to sink them into my soft lower belly.

"*Mine*," he whispers, before rising over me to kiss between my breasts, over my heart. "*Mine*." He grazes my skin with his beard, until his lips whisper against my own, "*Mine*." He presses his forehead to mine as he breathes me in with another definite hum of approval.

He gathers me into his arms and carries me upstairs, to my bathroom, where he showers the grape soda from my skin, but barely rinses his cum from between my legs.

I'm laid out on my bed, kissed and cherished, and rubbed down like a hard-working animal after a long day in the field.

"Tell me I can fuck you in your sleep," he whispers in

my ear, as my eyes grow too heavy for me to keep open. "Tell me I don't have to wait until the morning to be inside you again."

A lazy smile graces my lips. "I'm all yours, Daddy. Take good care of me."

EPILOGUE — GUNNAR
(EIGHT MONTHS LATER)

"I love it here," Jem says with a pretty sigh, tilting her head back to enjoy the evening sun on her face, as she bounces Viv on her knee.

My smile is automatic. "I'm glad." I clear the last of the suppertime cheese platter from the outdoor table, since her dads went home and we seem to be done with everything but the grapes. David and Gabe quite like our mountain home too, and they come for dinner at least once a week. Sometimes more, which Jem always seems surprised about.

Obviously her dads have more work to do, if they're going to convince her how much she really means to them. They miss her like crazy, now that she's not right next door to them, but the young woman who felt alone and rejected will need more time before she can trust the truth.

The fact that they make the effort to visit so often is starting to convince her though, and I'd never ask them to come less often. A girl needs her father. Or fathers.

Family to protect her and make her feel safe and capable and special.

I return my gaze to Viv, so chubby and happy. Well cared for. Our little girl is getting bigger. She's walking on her own these day, and I love to see her cruising around the garden, using the rock walls of the raised beds, to keep her balance when she's stealing strawberries.

I take a grape from the cheese platter, bite it in half, so it's not so big she could choke on it, and offer her one of the pieces, while I eat the other. She takes it from me with a grin, her eyes sparkling.

"Thank you?" I suggest.

"Takoo, Daddoo," she says, showing me how fucking smart she is before shoving the grape in her mouth with a flat hand. It falls out, and she stares at it on the ground, her lower lip pouting. She looks up at me with moist eyes as she points at it.

"It's okay, Sweet Pea. Look." I hold up another grape, bite it in half, and feed it to her directly.

Sadness forgotten, she sucks at it and grins at me again. She's so fucking cute, I can't help grinning back.

"You are so bleeping sexy when you *dad* our kid, Gunnar Scott." Jem shifts in her seat and opens her mouth for a grape of her own.

"Did you just use *dad* as a verb?" I chuckle and bite a grape, to share with her too. I could give her a whole one, but I like this better. I push it between her barely parted lips, and she suckles at my finger, before I pull it away.

I stroke her soft skin where her cropped Metallica T-shirt leaves her sexy-as-fuck growing bump on display, and then squeeze her hip in a more aggressive and suggestive way. "Better watch yourself, or I'll bleeping *daddy* you so hard, I'll turn that baby in your belly into twins."

Jem laughs until she snorts. "That's not how it works."

"I know, but it's something I like to think about," I say with a smile, before I take the food inside and tidy the kitchen.

When I head out again, Jem has Viv asleep at one breast, and her T-shirt is pushed up to reveal her other big, dark nipple. Her hair is shining, her skin is glowing, her gorgeous baby bump is on full display, and the sight of such a fertile goddess, blessing this fucking garden, makes me want to worship at the shrine between her thighs.

My mouth is fucking watering as I walk over, and I pull my chair right up close, needing a front-row seat to this picture of utter bliss.

Her belly has grown so fast. I fucking love the shape of her, and I'm so grateful I get to partake in the wonder this time. One of my favorite tasks is rubbing cocoa butter all over her stomach, because for some reason, Jem hates the idea of getting more stretch marks. I don't really understand her issue with them. The faded ones are evidence of how beautifully she carried Viv, and they're kind of my only connection to that time. She doesn't believe me when I tell her I love them, but I do.

She's gained a few stretch marks this time around, and she scowls at every single one when it appears. Obviously, the lotion isn't fully effective in preventing them, which bugs the hell out of Jem, but I think we both adore the moisturizing ritual, so we keep it up daily, while I secretly celebrate each new pink streak on her skin as it arrives. I can't feel any other way when they're basically the physical manifestations of my desires. She's growing my baby inside her, and I couldn't be more smitten or obsessed. She's fucking perfection.

Double-checking the baby's asleep, I unbutton my jeans and sit with my cock in my hand, stroking it as Jem gives me a knowing smirk.

She spreads her legs, showing me what she's wearing under her short summer skirt — *nothing*.

Bare and beautiful, she glistens with arousal, and I grip the hair on my chest the way she sometimes does, and tug as my cock strains in my fist.

"You're so fucking pretty, Jemma Scott. I can't believe you let me marry you and fuck you on the daily. You're bearing my beautiful babies, making sure they get all your soft goodness too, and we're all fucking lucky to have you. You know that, don't you?"

Jem rolls her eyes at me, and I rumble at her, "Tell me you fucking know how special you are, little wife."

"I'm super special." She doesn't sound the least bit convinced.

"You think you can placate me with sarcasm and disbelief, Miss?" I ask in a warning tone. "Tell me what you think I see."

She twitches her eyebrows and looks down at herself. "A good mom?"

"A fucking great mom," I correct her. "What else?"

She runs her tongue over her teeth and spreads her legs more widely, as her sweet lips curl higher on one side. "A series of tight little holes you like shoving your cock into?"

"A series of tight little holes I fucking *love* shoving my cock into. What else?"

Her brows lower into a deep, pensive V. "A good daughter?"

"The *best* fucking daughter two dads could ever wish for. What else?"

She pauses, like she needs time to think about it. "A smart, creative human?" she says eventually, as if it may not be true.

I lean closer. "The smartest, business-savviest, most creative entrepreneur I ever heard of. Pulling in six figures before the age of twenty and knowing that's only the beginning because you love what you fucking do, and there's a whole world out there waiting to praise you for it. You're special as fuck, and everyone fucking knows it and wants to invest in you. Tell me how many followers you have."

"Two-point-four-million," she says, her cheeks growing pinker by the second.

"How many offers from production teams?"

"Three."

"Tell me which other woman you know, does all that while raising beautiful babies and keeping her husband so fucking satisfied he can't think a single thought beyond her and the family she's given him."

"Zero," she mumbles, her head low.

I lean closer and pull my ear forward. "I'm sorry. *How* many people are as amazing as my brilliant wife?"

"None," she admits, though quietly.

"Exactly. You're the only one we know, and that makes you pretty fucking special. Ask Viv. You think she knows anyone as amazing as you?"

"Maybe one." Jem looks me over, her eyes full of approval, as she drinks me in.

I grunt at the compliment and shake my head at her. "I'll keep working on you. One day, you'll see what I see. A beautiful girl with a big brain and a big heart. A fun and loving woman with a gorgeous body, and a warrior's attitude. Nurturing mother of beautiful children, pride and joy of her parents—"

"Needy and wanton receiver of her husband's cock," she interjects. "Filthy wildcat in the sack, and wet as fuck for a man who won't quit making her feel embarrassingly over-glorified." She kicks her flip-flop at me, and then lifts Viv to her shoulder, to rub our baby's back. "Put this sleeping baby to bed, so you can play with me, Daddy."

"In a minute, Little Miss." I lean back in my chair, stroking myself some more while I take in every pretty thing about her. The baby, the bump, the wet pussy, and the huge fucking tits I keep sucking to keep her milk in supply, now that Viv needs less of it.

"Your T-shirt slipped down a bit. Lift it for me, so I can see your tits better," I command, loving how thick her nipples have become with her pregnancy hormones and all the feeding.

Jem does as she's told, her fingertip tracing the perimeter of the darker skin surrounding her nipple. Her areolae are larger and more defined than when we first met — another sign I've made my mark on her body, and I love it. I also love how fucking indecent it feels to take as much of them as I can into my mouth when I suck at her.

Mindful of my obsession, she teases her nipple to a proud salute.

"Milk it," I demand in a husky voice.

She wraps her palm around the side of her large breast and massages, encouraging milk forth with her thumb and fingers. It drips to her round belly, and she shivers as it trickles down her side.

"Your skirt has dipped, and it's covering you too much." My voice cracks with need. "Spread your legs wider."

She does so, showing me how much she's enjoying herself — she's slicked her upper thighs with shine.

"So fucking beautiful. Imagine how fucking special I must feel, knowing I get to love all of this." I draw a circle in the air with my finger, framing my favorite view.

I push myself up from my chair, tuck my cock away, step close to kiss Jem's soft lips, and then carefully lift our sleeping angel into my arms.

"I'm going to be back in five minutes, and if you're not too tired, you're going to be ready for me."

"I'll be ready and willing," she says with a secretive smile. She props her foot on her chair and parts her folds, for me to see her cunt blowing me kisses.

A long, strained moan of appreciation lingers in my throat, and I turn around and head inside, to put Viv to bed.

When I get back outside, Jem is naked and kneeling with her legs apart, on the big, solid-wood tabletop that she's covered with a thick blanket.

Bless the fucking mountainous countryside and its lack of fucking neighbors.

Her head is bowed, and her hands are behind her back, already slipped into the leather restraining cuffs we use sometimes, when she wants one of us to be strapped to the bed.

A length of black, shiny rope loops through her cuffs, to bind her to the far table legs. She's moved into position after anchoring herself, and there's not a lot of slack in the rope.

"Well, looky-here." I let out a low whistle, as I move to stand in front of her. "Seems I've caught a fertile little mama in my snare. She looks like a keeper, too. Pretty as a picture. Sexiest fucking hood ornament this table's ever had."

Jem giggles, and I slip my finger under her chin, to thrust her face up so I can see it. "Young. Maybe too young for this old country boy, but — mm-*mm* — you're cute as fuck, and curvy to boot."

I slide my hand between her parted thighs and use two fingers to capture her clit and rub it in slow circles. "Are you my type, baby girl? Wet and ready to take my big cock at a moment's notice?"

Jem utters a soft gasp, as I thrust my fingers inside her slick heat. I probe and push at her walls. "Going to have to stretch you enough to fit, but I'll make sure you take me."

Her pussy slurps at my fingers, and she shivers. I fuck

them in and out of her a few times before bringing them in front of my face. "You made my whole hand shine so prettily. You'll take my fat cock just fine." I suck her juices noisily from my fingers. "Mmm... Just a whole lot of sweet and ripe, aren't you, pudding? Good for breeding — that's for damn sure."

I trail the tip of my finger from her hairline, down her nose, between her breasts, and over the bulge of her belly. "About six months along, I reckon. Ready for breeding again, in about four or five—"

Jem clears her throat loudly, and I smile.

"Maybe six more months," I say. "Guess I could give your little body a rest before, I fuck another one into you. Grow my brood."

I use my damp fingers to trace the curve of her fullest breast.

The way her hands are bound behind her back makes her chest is thrust high and forward. I can't resist the temptation, and she knows it. She fucking loves it when I massage and suckle her milky breasts.

"Good set of teats on you." I give one nipple a little tug, and then more of a milking pull, until breastmilk beads on the tip. "Looks like I've got a little milker on my hands. Going to be a good girl and feed my babies? Grow 'em good and strong?" I milk her until she's antsy and restless and whimpering. "Going to feed me during the long cold winters?" I latch on and swallow down her spray when the letdown hits.

Jem rocks on her knees and leans toward my tugging mouth. Her binds draw tight, and she whimpers as I suckle even harder, drinking her down like I have a thirst to quench.

I yank open my jeans, tear off my shirt, and run my hands over her body, basking in her round shape and the fact that *I* fucking did this to her.

I fucked her young body full of seed, and she grew me a baby.

Twice.

I wasn't there for her the first time, but I'm here now, and I'm not missing a fucking thing. I love every fucking change her body is going through, and I seriously can't get enough of her. She's my fruitful little mama, and I live and breathe to serve her.

One glimpse of her swollen belly or the sight of my baby at her breast is all it takes to get me hard.

Her young, supple body is wearing my child with grace and ease, and her curves have only grown curvier. She fills my hands with her softness, making it easy to admire the firmness of her expanding belly and the movements of the life she's baking within.

The baby presses against my hand, and I moan into her breast.

We created life together. What greater blessing could the universe place on our union?

I release my suction and let her slip from my mouth.

"I need to be inside you real soon, beautiful. You're too fucking pretty and good to me."

I look over her restraints and swear. "Back up. Give me some slack to work with."

She does what she's told, and I loosen the rope to allow her arms more movement. I work the rope under her, while I guide her to turn, so she's facing the other way with her wrists bound in front of her body instead.

"Better. Now get your ass back to the edge of the table. I need to fuck it."

She squeaks, and I shake my head. She finally managed to take my fat cock in her tight ass a few months ago, but no amount of lube kept her from feeling where I'd been. Apparently, she's not too eager to be walking like a cowgirl again.

"Promise I won't fuck your asshole." I chuckle. "Just park your hindquarters where I can fuck that pretty young cunt of yours until you come, Little Miss."

Jem backs her ass to the end of the sturdy table and flashes me a grin. "Yes, Daddy."

I press a kiss to her head, shorten her tether to remove the slack, and secure it again.

"You could fuck it a little," she says with a sweet smile. "Just not with anything as big as your cock."

I bow my head in gratitude and pull the smaller of her glass dildos from my back pocket. The short one with a bulb at the tip, another bulge midway, and a flared base. "How about this?"

Her mouth makes an O shape, and I steal a quick kiss before moving behind her.

She gasps and shivers when I drip lube onto her asshole, and I press the very tip of the glass cock to her puckered ring, to barely breach her. "I'm going to hold this right here. Feel free to use it, while I do this."

I spank her lightly, right on the pussy lips, then strum her clit until she starts rocking her hips the way I like.

She nudges her ass back against the dildo, taking the first bulge inside her ass with a needy moan.

I give it a twist and a flick, then leave it stuck there, while I check the tension on her binds, and then spank her clit and rub it again. "There's more waiting for you, little mama."

Her thighs quiver, and her pretty little cunt is starting to drip with arousal. It's making her fine curls damp, and I love how they get extra curly when that happens.

I lower my mouth to her sex, part her pussy lips with my hands, and kiss her cunt long and deep until she's moaning good and low. I slowly pull back, and she chases my retreat.

Her binds pull fast, preventing her from coming any closer, and I flick the tip of my tongue at her, teasing until she's rocking her pelvis in an attempt to reach me. I work the second bulbous knob of the ass toy toward her, stretching her tightest hole in a tease, but not pushing it deeper.

"You want it? Spread your knees so you're lower, and you'll get more give."

Jem obeys, and I praise her like the good fucking girl she is.

I shove the ass plug inside her to the hilt, grab her hips, and bury my face in her pussy, until she gets twitchy and vocal, begging me to let her come.

"You put yourself in restraints, and that means Daddy's in charge, beautiful. You'll come when I tell you to come." I spank her ass, and she clenches around the sex toy as she cries out.

I spread her folds and stare at her juicy, dripping cunt. "Blow a kiss for Daddy."

She squeezes her core, and her pussy smacks a kiss at me, while the plug in her ass bobs up and down.

"Mmm... Again," I command. She does as I ask, three more times, and I let my head fall back with a moan. "Too fucking cute." I slap her ass, stand behind her, and drag the fat head of my cock through her slick.

She's at just the right height to be fucked.

She strains against her cuffs when she feels me at her entrance, and if the juices she's dousing me with are anything to go by, she's anxious for my cock to be inside her.

"Move forward an inch," I command.

She does so, and I follow her, staying pressed hard against her opening, but not pushing inside. "Show me you want it. Take what you want. What you can."

She rocks her hips against me, as I hold my cock firm, and slowly but surely she works her tight cunt over the broad head of my cock until her pussy lips are pulled taut, her ass is twitching, and she's panting like a woman in labor.

She bucks back at me as far as she can, and I moan, as the thick bloom of my cock enters her hot, snug channel. "Good girl, Little Miss. Now fuck Daddy's cock," I rumble, stroking her back and grinding my palm on the flared base of the toy in her ass. A gorgeous fucking friction occurs when its bulbous knobs massage my cock through her thin inner walls.

Jem moans long and loud, as she ripples around me,

swaying on all fours and tilting her pelvis to take more of my massive dick.

This is one of my favorite positions. She's always so fucking tight, and I love seeing her this stretched for me.

She braces her forearms on the tabletop and rocks on her knees, slowly at first, and then fast when her gushing cunt lubes the way. She gets so fucking wet for me, and hearing how slick she makes me is always so fucking hot.

I slap her ass, to egg her on, and she tugs at her binds as she impales herself on my cock without getting the full length.

Her movements speed up, and the friction on my cock is phenomenal, but my Little Miss is getting all worked up, because she needs something more, but she can't reach her clit when her hands are tied.

She pumps herself back and forth on my cock, and I hold myself in place, gritting my teeth, and bearing down with my abs, to keep from coming as my balls throb and tighten.

I slap her ass and then reach down and hold my fingers firmly to her clit. "Use them. Get what you need from me, beautiful."

She adjusts her angle and gets loud and moany, the way I like.

"That's it. Good girl. Use Daddy. Just like that."

Her cunt clamps more tightly, and I grunt and redouble my efforts to hold back my orgasm. I'm desperate to grab her hips and fuck her with savage abandon, but I forbid myself from doing it.

I don't fuck her too roughly when she's pregnant.

That's a breeding man's game, and she's already bred. I stroke her round belly and squeeze my abs even harder.

She's speeding up and grinding hard, and I nudge the toy in her ass so it's fucking her too.

That does it.

She goes off like a screaming rocket, her keening wails flushing birds from the trees and reverberating of the mountains surrounding us — "*Daddy.*"

Her cunt squeezes at me so hard, it feels like the knobby plug in her ass will leave an impression — and what a fucking impression, too. The pressure it applies to my cock makes her grip feel even stronger, and finally allowing myself movement, I gently push in and out of her contracting cunt, massaging my cock with those nodules until I spill into her depths with a ready groan.

Her spasms milk me beautifully, and I battle to stay upright when my balls are pulsing, my head is dizzy and tingling, and my fucking eyes are crossing from how fucking good it feels.

I grip the table and pull the toy from her ass, so I can stop seeing double. She presses her forehead to the table with a low, trembling whimper, and I ease my cock from her perfect heat, so I can watch her sweet young pussy drip my cum onto the blanket.

My beautiful wife. Round with child. Swollen little cunt, all fucked and seeded. No need for condoms ever again.

Just me and her. Always.

I pull the blanket up and over her back before releasing her from her restraints. I rub her wrists and check them over, to make sure she didn't hurt herself, then gather her into my arms and carry her spent body inside, to prep her for bed.

I feed her chocolate and strawberries in the shower, massaging any tight muscles with the slippery body wash, as I rub her down.

Jem insists on washing my cock. She does it with her mouth and gets herself some cream to swallow for those strawberries. I bundle her in towels and get her dried and tucked into bed. I check on Viv one last time before climbing in behind Jem and stroking her hair until she hums and closes her eyes, ready for sleep.

This has sort of become our nightly routine.

Jem loves her hair being stroked. It's always so soft and smells unbelievable, and it makes me feel happy and content to feel it beneath my fingers, like I'm petting a sexy kitten.

I think she likes it because it's reassuring, and my girl needs good, solid care, to be happy and feel safe, which is great, because that's my favorite thing to give her.

She came to me with that need, and I couldn't help but fulfill it, so our love languages are extremely compatible.

Being loved and cherished lights her up like nothing else, and to see her shine is a privilege.

She snuggles in, and then giggles when her ass butts up against my cock. "Does that pretty dick of yours ever go fully soft?"

"Around you? Impossible," I murmur tucking it out of her way. "Get some good sleep, beautiful," I whisper and kiss her head. "You're very busy and important, you know."

She snorts softly. "*You're* busy and important. You take care of me and Viv, and I don't know if you noticed, but we can be high maintenance."

I chuckle quietly near her ear. "You're both pretty vocal about what you want; I'll give you that. But mostly, you make me feel needed, and I like that."

"I definitely need you, Gunnar Scott. And I love you from top to toe."

"I love you too, Little Miss. Be sure to have sweet dreams. Your body is doing a lot of magic right now, and I know you're going to be wonderful all over again tomorrow, so you need to recharge this gorgeous little baby-making miracle well."

"Yes, Daddy." There's a smile in her voice, and she intentionally snuggles her ass right in against my hard cock, slotting the thing between her buns like a hotdog, before taking a deep breath and relaxing completely.

I nuzzle into her hair and kiss the back of her head, while I stroke her growing belly. "Good girl."

Daddies are important.

But a Daddy's girl is someone really special, and a good daddy makes sure she knows it.

AND THE YEAR AFTER THAT…

J em parks next to our minivan and climbs out of the
truck, wearing her self-labeled *smart-as-fuck business attire* and a huge grin on her face.

Her outfit is literally her Converse sneakers, jeans, a
T-shirt, and a tie — and she looks cute as hell. "It's offi-
cial," she says, shutting the truck door. She takes her
daughter from me as Viv reaches out and calls for her
mama.

Jem gives our girl a big smooshy kiss and cuddles her
close, before she leans to our son and blows a raspberry
on his cheek.

"They bought it?" I ask, shifting Tobin higher on my
hip, before I bend down to get my kiss.

Jem blows a raspberry on my cheek, too, making Viv
giggle, and then kisses me properly on the lips. "Yup.
Daddoo and Me is going to air in the living rooms of kids
from seventeen different countries," she says, bouncing
on the spot.

I bounce too, and Viv thinks it's a party, so she cheers,

and even Tobin burbles and flaps and proudly shows off his new tooth.

I shake my head at my young wife in wonder. "Jem that's *amazing*."

"*You're* amazing. That studly, woolen rabbit-daddy is based on you, Daddoo."

"Little Viv Rabbit and her baby brother Tobes are the real stars," I say, my cheeks warming.

Jem looks me over. "Do I need to send you to the *Gunnar Scott School of Belief*, to improve your self-esteem?"

My cheeks blaze even hotter, and I shrug. "What are the classes like? Any good?"

Jem crooks her finger at me, so I'll bend close and she can whisper in my ear.

"It's mostly a lot of baby-making activities, a mixture of sweet-talk and-dirty talk, and a consistent, liberal application of love."

"Sounds hot," I whisper, stealing a kiss before switching Tobin to my other hip, so I can slip my arm around my girls and herd them inside. "Maybe I'll enroll. See what happens."

Jem snorts and lets a squirming Viv down, to run. Then she takes Tobin from me, tosses her tie over her shoulder, lifts her shirt, and latches the hungry boy on as she walks. "You're looking at what happens."

I nod in approval. "I like it. Sign me up."

"I want you to see the latest clip I made, first." She pulls her phone from her back pocket and works it one-handed, like a fucking whiz-kid. The things this woman can do with one thumb...

Jem points to the couch and waits for me to sit before handing me the phone. She settles next to me and makes faces at Tobin when he grins and gurgles at her tit about how happy he is that she's home. He adores her as much as the rest of us do, and for a moment, I just watch the two of them, my heart full.

Jem notices me staring and blushes. Her knee knocks into mine. "Push *Play*," she urges, her cheeks getting pinker the longer I stare at her.

I give an approving grunt and do what I'm told.

But it's not the cute clip of frolicking woodland creatures I was expecting.

For starters, instead of the light, and bouncy opening theme-song she normally uses, Jem's gone with a *bow-wow-chikka-chikka* that sounds more like a classic porn soundtrack, and the title that comes up reads, *Daddy and Little Miss*.

I stare at her, and she points at the phone, laughing. "You have to keep watching."

So I do.

I watch Daddoo Rabbit fucking Mama Rabbit in some very not-advisable-for-a-timid-audience positions.

"*Oh my God*. Is it bad that I'm getting hard?" I whisper, making sure Viv's not in the room, so I can watch without needing to shield my crotch and my phone from her on account of her mother's fucking next-level-obscene creativity. "I'm never going to be able to look at Daddoo Rabbit the same way again. You've stolen my innocence. What the hell position is... *Oh fuck*." I laugh and shake my head at Jem. "We did that one last month. Made a fucking impression, did it?"

Jem simply smiles, takes hold of my chin, and directs it back toward the screen, urging me to keep watching.

Daddoo Rabbit keeps fucking Mama, but something's happening. It looks as if Jem's added more stuffing to Mama Rabbit throughout the sequence — to her belly.

Daddoo got his Little Miss pregnant with all that fucking — and he keeps going at her in all sorts of ways until she looks fit to burst her stuffing.

The shot leaves their raunchy little bedroom stage and moves into a much sweeter nursery. Then there's a shot of some little bunny babies, sleeping in their little woolen beds while the proud Daddoo and Mama Rabbit watch over them. A young one with blonde curls and a blue bow; a smaller, darker-haired one, holding a teddy bear just like Tobin's; and a new, tiny little baby bunny that I've never seen before.

I lower the phone and stare at Jem.

Her smile is so fucking pretty, I want to take her upstairs and do about sixteen of the fucking things Daddoo Rabbit did to Miss.

"You're pregnant?" I whisper, my heart fluttering as much as the butterflies in my stomach.

She presses her smiling lips together and nods.

I grip the back of her head and bring her mouth to mine in a hungry, overexcited kiss, before launching off the couch and pacing one way, and then the other. "We need to celebrate. And delete that fucking thing off your phone before Viv sees it." I throw my hands up; that was too hasty. "*No.* Send it to me. I want it. Fuck, I can't believe you did that. It's fucking brilliant, and so fucking warped, in the hottest way." I tug at my hair and groan.

"Where do I keep it? On a pen drive, in the locked box of naughty things in the closet?"

"Who has a fucking pen drive in this day and age?" Jem asks, giggling. She pats the spot next to her on the couch. "Sit your ass down, boomer. Take a breath. You're happy?"

I sit down, unable to keep my eyes off her. "*Happy?* I'm fucking ecstatic." I kiss her again, so she understands exactly how pleased I am, and leave her on the couch, feeding Tobin with a slightly dazed-looking expression on her face.

"We definitely need to have a party," I call through the house. I walk past the playroom, and wave at Viv to follow me. "*Viv*, Mama's going to have another baby. Help your studly Daddoo find the balloons."

NEED MORE?

Thanks for reading
WILD OAT MILK

I follow my erotic muse wherever that filthy bitch takes me so each story I write can be quite different from the last — but I always aim for a certain level of sweetness to accompany some extreme fucking heat, and *all* of my stories are written to *satisfy*.

Try another... if you dare.

X

BOOKS BY ELENA DAWNE...

Mountain Daddy's Milk and Honey

Mountain Daddy's Milk and Honeymoon

Wild Oat Milk

Her Mountain Man Beast

The Mountain Man's Sugar Shack

A Brat for the Mountain Giant

Mountain Santa's Naughty List

Daisy Unchained

Intolerant

Untold Restraint

ABOUT THE AUTHOR

Elena Dawne is the "super-secret" pen name of some author chick who likes to dive into some good old-fashioned smut to cleanse her palate between projects. Does she have a kink preference? No. Elena's enjoyed so many different types of erotica she no longer knows where her limits are. She just writes whatever the fuck she thinks is hot and fun, then shares it with y'all.

Erotica is her energy-boosting rebound juice when life is just too fucking serious — not alone there, right? ;)

If you want to tell her what you think of her books, you can do that via reviews or email her at elenadawne@gmail.com. To keep posted about her releases you can follow her on Amazon, Bookbub, or Facebook.

Thanks again for reading! X

Printed in Great Britain
by Amazon

38302669R00138